BORN-AGAIN VIOLENCE

We were face to face, panting somewhat. Being a lout practiced in loutish ways, he'd realized that if he struggled he could end up with two broken wrists, courtesy of a brother lout.

Now for the chancy bit. I wasn't standing here all night holding the Reverend's bodyguard. Any instant, there'd be other bodyguards to the rescue. In any event, it'd been a while since I told anyone, "Promise to be good if I let you go?"

THE
MAN
AT THE WHEEL

Michael Kenyon

AVON BOOKS ◆ NEW YORK

AVON BOOKS
A division of
The Hearst Corporation
105 Madison Avenue
New York, New York 10016

Copyright © 1982 by Michael Kenyon
Published by arrangement with Doubleday & Company, Inc.
Library of Congress Catalog Card Number: 82-45397
ISBN: 0-380-70381-5

First Avon Books Printing: May 1988

AVON TRADEMARK REG. U.S. PAT. OFF. AND IN OTHER COUNTRIES, MARCA REGISTRADA, HECHO EN U.S.A.

Printed in the U.S.A.

K-R 10 9 8 7 6 5 4 3 2 1

ONE

My name is Peter Ramsden. I am twenty-eight, a journalist, and I'm going to live.

The black, whispering policeman—I assume he's a policeman—has shown me the pellets they've taken out of me. His palm was creased and cinnamon-coloured, and the pellets lay there like a nest of grubs. He keeps coming and going, I don't know why. His voice is so hushed I can hardly hear him. If this is his bedside manner, I'm not ungrateful.

The doctor has the bedside manner of a potato, and his hands are cold. But he's on the side of life. He might even be the surgeon who operated. I don't know. They don't tell you anything. Today they've taken away the drip thing and let me have this tape recorder.

Eject—Stop—Play. It works, which is more than I do.

I want to get it down. The outline, rough notes as it were, though eventually there must be a book in it. Not the sort of book I ever saw myself writing, but there we are.

This is Orville Faubus Ward. A long way from home. I don't know what the date is but it's not Christmas yet because Mr. Crosby is still dreaming about his white one, except when the massed cherubim interrupt with Rudolph and his shiny nose. With luck I could be back in London by Christmas. They don't tell you yes, no, or even perhaps.

Too weak for more now. I can't feel most of my body. Nothing in either leg. When I hold the honourable male member for Manchester North there's no feeling there either, it's like holding air, which came as a shock. I doubt I'll be throwing hammers in the next Olympics. A party is what I'm going to throw when I get home, to celebrate life, because I'm going to live.

I think the other copper, the London one—Peckover, is it?—may be going to die. He's here somewhere, or he was. He may have died already. The whispering policeman wouldn't say. Neither would Dr. Chilly Fingers. For the world's most open society, they're as open as oysters here. I suppose hospitals are the same everywhere.

I was born in Manchester, and from Manchester Grammar went to Manchester University, where I wrote, debated, and acted. Modesty, I've always believed, is a virtue, but a modest virtue. I see no point in belittling my command of the Queen's English, or the fact that nature has favoured me in respect of looks. Onstage I'm an adequate presence whether in doublet and hose or top hat. I knew everyone at university. I went to a thousand parties, cut a thousand lectures, and barely scraped through my finals.

No matter. My aim has never been to become an academic or Her Majesty's ambassador in Tokyo. I intended to write plays for the West End and Broadway. In the meantime, for a living, it was going to have to be journalism. Logically, the first step should've been *The Manchester Guardian*, or plain *Guardian*, as it became when it shunted to London about the time I was born. I'd have preferred the London office, having outgrown Manchester, but I was willing to accept Manchester if there were no immediate vacancy in London.

There was no immediate vacancy, period. Get some experience and come back in a year or two though we can't make promises, they said. *The Times, Telegraph,* posh Sundays, and cerebral weeklies said the same. I applied to the BBC. I filled in the forms, attended an interview, and received a regretful letter saying that due to cutbacks, et cetera. Ditto, commercial television, which I'd never regarded as me anyway, though occasionally it puts out a superior programme.

Of course, this was the start of the recession, and employers were nervous.

I wrote off the reverses, lowered my sights, and tried the bigger provincial papers. Leeds, Liverpool, Glasgow, Birmingham, Bristol, Sheffield, so on.

"Dear Mr. Ramsden, Thank you for your inquiry . . . Unfortunately . . . We have filed your application and in the event that . . ."

One editor, chattier than the others, wrote that untrained, inexperienced, in spite of my university activities and obvious ability, I'd be useless to any editor, while still having to be paid at the union rate, so it was not going to be easy, but good luck.

About now, the first unbelievable crawlings of panic. I'd heard of unemployment and seen it, which is to say I saw it daily, but unemployment had always been for other people.

My sights sank ignominiously through the floor. In the reference room at the Central Library in St. Peter's Square I wrote to forty-seven newspapers, drawing the line only at gutter rubbish and such hopeless cases as the Llanflanfach *Weekly Countryman.* For two months I watched for the postman while slaving in my dad's bakery. Then I started writing to newspapers in Canada, Australia, New Zealand, Bermuda, anywhere where the language was English. The Jamaica *Gleaner* replied that they'd be pleased to see me if I happened to be passing through Kingston, though they could guarantee nothing.

I was trying to make my name free-lancing, firing off stories and features which I worked on in the afternoons, knackered after half the night and all morning in the bakery. "Apathy in Academe: The Politics of Indifference." "Fellini, A Reappraisal." "Bread: Our Plastic Staff of Life." Nothing was accepted.

Eight months after graduating I was beginning to wonder if I was finished before I'd begun. What a little pond, the university! What a frozen ocean, life outside! If I'd had the money I might've paid a newspaper to take me on, as happened in the old days, but the only source of money was my dad, and he had views about scribblers who couldn't stand on their own feet after three years of university. I'm part idealist, part Bohemian, but I've never underestimated the importance of money.

I brooded on stopgaps. Salesman, swimming-pool attendant, the North Sea oil rigs. The bakery earned me my beer and cinema money, but it was never employment, it was family drudgery, and my life was in suspension. Then I remembered a girl friend from my second year at university.

She was Marjorie Heap, a biologist, plumpish, and fun except in bed, where she was too much fun, being always overtaken by the giggles. There're limits, and they're gone beyond when you know you're competent and the girl starts by tittering and eventually is bouncing about hysterical with laughter. Incredibly, Marje ditched me for a first-year engineer, but you couldn't stay cross with Marje. We remained on amiable terms. Her father, I recalled, late in the day, was a newspaper proprietor somewhere in the west country.

I remember remembering this while spading in the Viennese loaves at five o'clock on a March morning. I suppose I'd remembered sooner because the information had been too trivial when Marje had mentioned it, presumably in a lull between laughing fits. Good God, had it come to this? A potty seaside weekly? I didn't know *its* name, and assuming it's been listed in the reference library, I'd missed it precisely because it'd been too potty to consider.

Eastleigh-on-Sea was a dozy watering place of seven thousand dozy inhabitants, most of them a hundred years old. An escape car would whisk you out of it to Burnham-on-Sea or Weston-super-Mare, but once you were there, where were you? Fleeing in any other direction took you deeper into nowhere. Taunton, Lynton, Watchet, Glastonbury, no question they're fine if you're retired from life, or a hiker, or a horse, but for tomorrow's Tom Stoppard—Tom Stoppard had started out as a reporter in Bristol—one who'd seen himself filling in by covering world affairs for *The Guardian* or *The Times*, North Somerset came as a jolt.

The Eastleigh-on-Sea & District *Weekly Examiner* (Estb.

1892, Incorporating the Halscomb *Echo*) circulated in all directions including out to sea, there being a shipping page which told of tides and ship movements and was essential reading among shipping people, according to the shipping correspondent. The editorial staff numbered around eight or ten, and one more with my arrival. I say "around" because it was hard to be exact when departments overlapped and everyone doubled and quadrupled in assorted roles. The shipping correspondent, for example, also looked after layout, football and cricket, a gourmet column, and gymkhanas. The advertising manager wrote the editorials, council news, and the children's column (Uncle Alec). Arthur Tregunter, an *Examiner* staff man for forty-eight years, covered agriculture, motoring, chess, the arts, and wrote the financial page and obituaries. Everyone pitched in grudgingly with routine reporting while guarding their specialties. Everyone was expected to turn a hand to everything. That was one reason I'd tried to avoid a weekly, having no yen to be a contemporary Caxton, a frontier printer blind to everything beyond the immediate community, trudging from shopkeeper to shopkeeper soliciting advertising, and campaigning against lavatories on the esplanade.

I'd guess the point of a local paper was to be local, but I'd not realised how local. Mrs. G. Tiverton, of 24 Acacia Avenue, winner in the dahlias category, took precedence over the outbreak of war. Ronald Parrot, aged eight, twisted his ankle in the playground, received more column inches than an earthquake or a moon landing.

The proprietor, Colonel R. W. Heap, started to explain this parochialism when he invited me to tea at his home on the day I started. But he lost interest. He was a shy stick of a man—not at all like his daughter—whose enthusiasm was his silkworms. I never saw him again. He never came into the *Examiner*, leaving its running to the editor, Norman Stibbs.

Stibbs resented me from the start. He resented my university degree. I believe he resented my accent, or rather the absence of accent, because my speech would not be out of place at the National Theatre, though I've been told a hint of Lancashire is detectable if I become excited. What was unusual about my accent was that it was the only one of its kind on the *Examiner*, or come to that in Eastleigh, where the natives spoke with a bucolic burr. Stibbs made it plain that I might've been a big man at the university, but here I was a mistake, and though another's influence had brought me here, he was in a position to sack me. Every piddling job which was likely to lead nowhere, or at best to a solitary paragraph, he passed to me.

He passed me the chore of telephoning round the police and fire stations and hospitals, the trivial weddings, funerals of nobodies—if there were somebodies in Eastleigh, I never met them—chimney fires, traffic accidents where no one was hurt and the vehicles barely bruised, and presentations of clocks to retiring postmistresses. I'd stand all day in the rain watching the young farmers' hedge-trimming competition for a three-line intro and two columns of results, and sit all evening through the annual general meeting of the Gilbert and Sullivan Society. In time I learned the shortcuts, the names of chairpersons and secretaries from whom the same paragraph might be picked up by telephone. But Stibbs never hinted at shortcuts or helped in any way. Fair enough. This was the experience which in six months was going to take me to Fleet Street. Six months was my deadline for the *Examiner*.

Stibbs apart, the staff were genial, as well they might be considering that all the dross which they'd shared was now unloaded onto me. "See you're down for the Thorney Magna Thespians in *White Cargo*," Arthur Tregunter, theatre critic, would say over a pint in the Crown. "Sorry, old son, but I'm getting too long in the tooth for these sorties into the wilderness."

In one two-week spell I covered eight plays by amateur groups, each in a far-flung, unheated church where the audience numbered fifteen and from which the last bus back to Eastleigh would leave about nine, during the first interval—if I were lucky. There was no question of criticism. The *Examiner* rule was that every name on the programme be mentioned. Some players might be praised, but none damned.

The banknotes and coins in my weekly khaki envelope took care of my rent and nourishment with nothing over. I had a basement bed-sitter next to the bingo hall, which was closed from October to May, as was all other entertainment in the town, and hither I brought sundry local damozels, discovering anew that we gentlemen of the press, we roistering, hard-living, world-weary newspapermen, do have glamour even in Eastleigh-on-Sea. I rarely wined and dined them, or took them out. I didn't have a car, and while I'm as much in favour of gallantry as I am of women's lib, some of these girls were paid as much as I was, even the mere typists.

For the most part this apprenticeship was a mix of frustration, slogging, and fear of the axe for falling into the ultimate sin of getting the mayor's initials wrong. My only gross error—killing off a hospital patient who was very much alive—happened a year after I'd started, and created less of a stir than I'd have expected.

For want of demand on the part of Fleet Street I'd had no choice but to extend my six-month deadline. A mellower Stibbs was passing me stories which were not total zeros, though I still received much of the garbage, including the hospital calls. Fortunately there were no lawsuits, Robert Long, the spark with the broken arm whom I wrote up as dead, being tickled pink to read his death notice. The deceased was a nonagenarian Robert Long who'd languished in the same hospital for years, and the muddle was more the hospital's fault than mine. We carried a correction and apology, and the incident was buried along with the dead Mr. Long.

The incident which led to my leaving the seaside for the Smoke, the Big Time, and very nearly, seven years later, to my own burial here in Little Rock, took place a year and a week after I'd joined the *Examiner*.

I wasn't even on a job. I should've minded by own business. But pretty well anything might be a reporter's business, and I was acquiring a nose for news. News for the Eastleigh-on-Sea & District *Examiner* was whatever touched on Eastleigh-on-Sea. The opinion of outsiders, for example, so long as it was reasonably favourable. And here in the Crown were four authentic Arabs, lacking only falcons. They were besheeted, burnoused, and unsuitably sandalled. The force eight which had been blowing for two days was almost certainly going to be the week's headline.

They were filing from the dining room. At the bar, heads turned, mine among them. Phil Cole had been with me, but he'd left to cover a caged birds show, or a curate's ordination, so I was on my own, half into my second pint. Unless these sheiks were known to the *Examiner* and had already been tackled by whoever was our Middle East expert, I might have a story.

What were they doing here and what did they think of Eastleigh? What did they think of the Crown? Were they buying it? If they weren't, what were they buying, or were they penniless, and what'd they had for lunch? Names, ages, occupations, where they were from, where they were going, and any amusing, unusual experiences pertaining to Eastleigh. In my earliest trainee days, whatever time was available before an interview I'd spend in writing out and rehearsing questions, gnawing my nails, and screwing my courage to the sticking place. After a year and a week, no problem.

My first reaction was to go ahead. They might be worth half a column, if they spoke English.

My second reaction was balls to it. The *Examiner* paid nothing extra for any story I might bring back off my own bat, and I'd reached the resentful stage where I believed I was worth considerably more than my pittance. The robed quartet had already billowed out into the street. To catch them I'd have to gulp my beer, and for what?

Reaction number three. Though I'd not be paid for the story, if there were one, it'd bump up my expenses. Hospitality for Gulf visitors, £9.75. "Hospitality" was our expense-sheet euphemism for booze. There'd be no shelling out for booze either because I'd beard them on the pavement.

Outside the Crown, buttoning my raincoat to the neck, I failed to see them.

I tried left, to the esplanade, where they might be

checking into or out of our one two-star hotel. The sea was bashing against the sea wall, tossing spray high over the railings. Sea gulls which had chosen the sky rather than shelter were being buffeted every which way. Stepping out, I remembered that Arabs didn't booze—did they? I'd hardly recoup the cost of the shoe leather pretending I'd bought them lime juice.

Anyway, here I was, and there they were, climbing into a car parked a dozen paces away on the rain-swept esplanade. I scurried. The last of the four was stepping up into what was not a routine car but one of those long, sleek, airport limousine jobs which you don't realise the length and sleekness of until you see it side-on. They usually have Peter Stuyvesant or Wimbledon Tennis emblazoned on their flanks, though this one was plain, if plain's the word. Devonshire cream colour with a shimmer speckled by Eastleigh rain and mud. The last of the caliphs had entered, just, into the interior plush when I got my foot inside the door. I could've reached out and startled him with a gentle goosing.

"Excuse me," I called, and the caliphs, sorting themselves out amid upholstery and travelling rugs, eyed me out of bearded, desert faces. "I'm with the *Examiner*." I now had both feet in the limousine. "Might I have a word? Anything at all you'd like to tell me about Eastleigh—your impressions?"

"Sorry, John," a voice behind me said. The voice couldn't say its "r's." It was more like, "Sowwy, John."

I'd probably have stepped down anyway but I wasn't given the chance. A gloved hand on my shoulder drew me back onto the kerb, and a second gloved hand insinuated in front to push the door shut. A peaked, cheese-cutter cap in velvety material was pulled down over pale blue eyes, and a tunic with a page-boy collar was getting wetter by the second in the rain. He had a black beard but he wasn't an Arab, and it wasn't much of a beard, although he was big and beefy enough. What I'm saying is the beard was a poor thing because it hadn't been trying long enough, not for want of the right chromosomes. He looked thirty-five or so, and not only an anachronism but an inaccurate anachronism. No Edwardian milord would've supported such a scrubby, debutante beard on his chauffeur, whose gear was nothing if not Edwardian, straight out of *The Go-Between*. The whiff of whisky on his breath would've delighted milord even less.

Not that I got much of a look or smell. If he were merely a chauffeur—and if he weren't a chauffeur, why did he dress like one?—he could start by behaving like a chauffeur, and stop trying to push around an accredited, card-carrying representative of the Fourth Estate.

I told him, "D'you mind? I'm the press. I'm having a word with these gentlemen. If I'm holding you up you'll just have to spurt a bit, later. All right?"

A gloved hand moved, there came a pressure on my breastbone, and a booted ankle hooked behind my ankle. I felt myself going so I punched, which was astonishing because, though not a pacifist, and as ready to defend myself as the next man, I'd never tried to hit anyone, or not since playground battles, aged ten. More astonishing, I didn't miss, I hit him in the mouth, I wasn't aware of having aimed at his mouth, or anywhere particularly, and I didn't see the punch land any more than I saw the fist which struck the side of my head. I didn't even know if it was a fist.

Next, I was lying on the pavement, bells in my head, needles in my hand, and tremolos of pain vibrating up from my bum, somewhere from the coccyx region. Winded too. I couldn't call out to the Arabs or for help from anyone.

Not that there was anyone on the esplanade. Out of season, Eastleigh is empty, and emptiest of all the esplanade with its terraced quarter mile of closed hotels and boardinghouses. Privately I expect I was glad of this. Worst of all would've been the humiliation of being seen supine on the pavement. I had a glimpse of speculative beards pointing at me through the limousine's windows, and the chauffeur with a hand to his mouth climbing into the driver's seat. By the time I'd managed to sit up, the vehicle was accelerating away, its tyres splashing through puddles, and I was staring after and hoping it and its occupants—its chauffeur anyway—would skid in a dozen circles, and into the sea.

I'm not prophetic. No knack of second sight or powers of voodoo. When I say I was all for the limousine plunging into the briny, that was the momentary hope of an upended charlie on the Eastleigh esplanade. But that's not too far from what happened.

I was too occupied with my sufferings to indulge in prophecies anyway. Once the aches and pains had sorted themselves into localities as distinct from the first, all-embracing numbness, the keenest pain seemed to be in the hand I'd punched with. A tooth, white and bloody, was lodged in the third joint of my forefinger, close to the knuckles. Most of the blood spreading over the finger was my own.

My impulse was to yell and shake the tooth free, as you might a wasp which has its sting in you. After a deep breath or two, I eased the tooth out, wrapped it in a Kleenex, and put it in my pocket.

The first I knew about what happened to the chauffeur and his passengers was the television news that evening. There was film of the sea washing over the clotted-cream limousine, on its roof at the rocky foot of a cliff near Pithley, forty miles from Eastleigh. Between them a police rescue team, the coast guard, and an RAF helicopter had recovered four bodies—"believed to be Arab visitors"—and as far as I could gather they weren't looking for any more. Four, they seemed to believe, was the lot. Two had been in the car, one had been thrown from the car onto the rocks, and some hours after the wreck had been spotted the fourth had been fished out of the sea.

Moments after the item ended I was on the telephone to Fleet Street. My contribution was: Where was the Fifth Man, the chauffeur, a bruiser with spooky blue eyes and a gap in his front teeth, at least until he got to a dentist?

TWO

City of Little Rock Police Department, Little Rock, Ark. 72201. December 6.

From: Commanding Officer, 1st Homicide Zone.

To: 1. Police Commissioner. 2. Commissioner of the Metropolitan Police, New Scotland Yard, London, England.

Subject: Statement of Detective Chief Inspector Henry Peckover, CID, New Scotland Yard (Illegal Immigration), as recorded and transcribed by P.O. Pamela Kremer, Shield No. 427, HQ (Admin) LRPD.

(From P.O. Kremer to Police Commissioner: With the agreement of Commanding Officer Brabant, I have edited out of the following transcript all extreme remarks of a personal nature addressed by Det. Chf. Insp. Peckover to myself. Excised remarks, recoverable if required, were of a facetious, mainly erotic nature uttered while the patient was feverish. I wish to state that in consideration of the patient's condition I do not intend to file a complaint. The statement is otherwise verbatim, received in seven sessions, Dec. 4–6, commencement and termination of each session indicated by sextuple spacing in accordance with Stenography Code 3g, Publication 9, Statements in Evidence.)

I'm dreaming of a white Christmas too, but whether it's going to be in this world or the next, God knows.

All I know is if I'd got Bing's voice I'd not be here, I'd be on the box, not about to be put in one. I'd be up there in front of the bleeding cameras dreaming of a white, pink, or polka-dotted Christmas, I wouldn't be fussy, whatever my public wanted, that's what I'd give them. I'd be there dreaming and droning and crooning.

Sorry. Name's Henry Peckover, Detective Chief Inspector, C Department, Scotland Yard, and this is my last will and testament. Well, why not? Might as well take advantage of the secretarial service while it's here, and very svelte and tasty, too.

I leave all my worldly goods and chattels, including rejected poems, Swiss bank deposits, and my collection of Greek statuary—that's a joke, keep it in, let the boys in the back room know he died with quips on his lips—to my wife, Miriam, bestest and loveliest in this or any other world. And to the baby, natch.

In case some spark takes that to mean the baby's name is Natch, his name's Sam. He's all right, too. Just tell him, if these are my dying words, tell him not to become a copper.

If these are my dying words they're not going to make it into the *Dictionary of Quotations*.

Sorry, posterity. Sorry, darling Miriam. I couldn't really help it. As the cook said when she turned the heat up too high under the plaice, then everything went black.

Tell Sam it's not obligatory to become a copper. He doesn't have to follow in his dad's footsteps. If he insists, tell him to try for an indoor job, like combing the dogs.

Sorry. The beginning's got to be the reporter Ramsden. Someone might've rumbled the Reverend sooner or later if Ramsden hadn't. Then again, they might not.

There it goes, the merest twinge, nothing. Are there no bullets to bite on? They had bullets at bloody Waterloo? Enough, though, for the moment, if it's the same to you, Pamela, beloved, dearest honeypot.

Wait. Here you are then. The dying words of Peckover the Poet. "Elegy in an Oxygen Tent." By Our 'Enry, Bard of the Yard.

Here died a London copper,
    An amiable cock,
Who came a proper cropper
    In a church near Little Rock.

When did the Arabs snuff it at Pithley? Six, seven years
ago? Before the Iranian Embassy business, but after
Balcombe Street, must've been, because I'd been shifted
out of antiterrorism by then. I was with Vice, giving up
cigarettes.

Doesn't matter, it's in the file. Didn't have much to do
with us anyway, not at that stage. The Somerset hayseeds
were taking care of it. They wanted us to tell them who the
snuffed ones were. Were they from London? Their banger
had a Kensington registration, hired from Ladbroke
Rentals—wait, hold everything.

Expunge "hayseeds," Pamela old love. If I meet any of
the Somerset brigade on the Golden Shore I don't want a
pitchfork through my foot.

Vice got the query because the deputy commander had a
bee about Arabs coming to Britain for one thing only, and if
they'd driven off the road at Pithley it was because they
were on their way to get it and were overexcited in anticipation. Alternatively, they hadn't been able to get it so
they were playing with themselves, or with each other, at
eighty miles an hour. What he thought they could get in
Somerset they couldn't get in London, I can't imagine, but
he may have known things about Somerset we didn't. He
used to say Vice should open a dossier on every gent who
stepped off a Saudi TriStar at Heathrow, and he passed us
the Pithley query.

I passed it to Terry Sutton. That's Detective Sergeant
Sutton, terror of the rugby scrums. Tied knots in more
vertebral columns than you've had hot dinners. He was
back by teatime with the Arabs' names, addresses, and
approximate incomes.

Whoever they were, they're in the file. They were in the
papers, too. Four plutocrats in the wink of an eye, they
caused a bit of a splash, pardon the expression. They'd
had suites at the Berkeley. That squelched the deputy

commander's theory about Vice because if you're in London for one thing only you don't find it at the Berkeley, not unless you smuggle it up the staff lift in a laundry basket. You can't have a glass of water at the Berkeley unless you're wearing a tie. Quite right, too. Not that they're not ultra-decent about it, I don't doubt.

The deceased had wives, aunts, and retinues of cousins out of sight and mind in service flats in Queen's Gate, fortunately, or we'd not have learned much. Terry Sutton didn't find the hotel wildly cooperative. Can't blame them, it wouldn't have been the cheeriest publicity, four of your customers driving off the top of a cliff. Other hand, it wasn't as if they'd gone to their maker on the premises. Botulism from the caviar. A whiff of legionnaire's disease.

Terry got the impression there wasn't a lot to know. They'd kept to themselves, our foursome. Didn't hold orgies or turn up the stereo too loud. They were out most of the time, touring, sometimes for days at a stretch. And what, you're about to ask, did they tour?

Mosques, Pamela, and Arab connections, whatever they might be. Probably we've a museum somewhere with Omar Khayyám's authentic book of verses underneath the bough. Sounds the sort of loot one of our Victorians might've brought back from his travels. Up to Edinburgh went our Arab quartet, down to Brighton. Don't ask me. I wouldn't have thought it'd take long to get through Britain's mosques. Anyway, a scholarly appetite for mosques doesn't explain why they drove into the drink.

They weren't drunk. The pathologist wouldn't be shaken on that. They'd had lunch somewhere called Eastleigh and drunk Coca-Cola. The weather was lousy though, rain cascading and visibility Stygian at three in the afternoon. The coroner found that their car went out of control on the greasy coast road. Misadventure. Dust into dust, and under dust to lie.

Can we take five, Pamela, mavourneen? I think I'd like to die now.

I was saying we didn't learn much from the hotel. Even

less from the family, locked away like embarrassing se-
crets in the slums of Queen's Gate.

Pamela, pet, don't you ever react? That was irony. Even
a girl from Little Rock must know Queen's Gate is swish.
Albert Hall way, right? Robert Browning lived in De Vere
Gardens. Got his plaque up on the wall.

Forget it.

One reason we didn't learn much from the family retinue was that two days after the mishap at Pithley they
scarpered. The entire tribe, back to the sandy wastes and
bubbling oil, taking with them four coffins, and the flesh
therein barely cold. Precipitate, some of us were wont to
aver, not to say irregular, but their embassy was in a
position to cut corners because who're we to dispute with
the sheikdoms? Nothing suspicious about it though. They
simply wanted to go home.

Why Terry learned nil on his first trip to the service flats
was that none of them spoke English. Took him the best
part of a day to unearth an interpreter. We're not strong on
languages at the Factory—the Yard—and their embassy
didn't want to know. I told him to try the Hilton, where
the air crews from Kuwait and Qatar shack up, so in he
breezed and coaxed a steward out of bed. I'd be coaxed
out of bed if someone with the bulk of Terry Sutton were
doing the coaxing. Back at Queen's Gate, all the women
were wearing their black drapes. None of them would say
a word, not even through the interpreter, though they
giggled a lot. Terry thought the jollity out of place,
considering.

The uncles and nephews were more forthcoming. What
they were forthcoming about was the repercussions if the
money in the possession of the four deceased at the time
of the misadventure wasn't handed back *presto*.

We asked around about this. They've got their own
Bank of Bahrain, and the Muscat and Oman First National
and all that in Gracechurch Street and Leadenhall Street,
but seems it's common for sheiks on the move to carry
their savings in handbags and tucked under their djellabas.
It's not compulsory, some use banks, perhaps the old-
fashioned ones, those who stepped from the sands to The

Sands in a weekend, but quite a few use envelopes. No money was found in the wreck, not a rial, dinar, or Bank of England oncer. None on the bodies or in their baggage. Course, it might've been washed out to sea, if there was any in the first place. Unlikely, because the uncles and aunts had accounted for all the possessions recovered from the car, including zipped-up moneybags, satchels, and briefcases. None of them contained a penny.

The uncles claimed the money had been nicked by the Somerset police. That didn't put Terry Sutton in the best of tempers. Apart from the slur, the charge was ludicrous to anyone who knows the Somerset force. I'm not saying they're rustics out there, perish the thought, but they're not in the big corruption league either. They might pocket a 50p picked up under the turnstile at a football game, but they'd not know where to begin with the sort of money the four sheiks were supposed to have been carrying. My opinion anyway.

For reasons best known to themselves the uncles had ordered the trunks of their dead brought from the Berkeley to the flat where Terry arrived with his interpreter. To keep an eye on them, probably. They weren't trusting anyone by this time. One of them got excited and started crying at Terry, "There'll be repercussions!"

Terry told him, "So you speak English. How many more of you speak English?"

This excitable one with his repercussions sounded to me more a nephew than an uncle because I gather he was only about nineteen. White suit, limbs a-jangle with gold bracelets. He said he didn't speak English. He began pulling open drawers in one of the cabin trunks, and throwing clothing and junk in the air, and shouting, "See, no funds! Always they took with them their funds! Your police are thieves! You will see, there will be repercussions!"

I don't too much like picturing Sergeant Sutton holding himself in. He's pink and blond, and when he's cross he goes pinker and blonder. When he's extremely cross he becomes a doughy colour. I'd hazard he'd have been the colour of pastry by now, standing there besieged by giggling draped photographers, socks and burnouses whirling through the air, and this jangling Fancy Dan in his white two-piece shrieking about repercussions. When Terry told him to calm down he switched to Arabic and started shaking his fists.

"Look, Ali Baba, don't you threaten me," Sergeant Sutton said.

He shouldn't have said that. Can't see anything too insulting about being called Ali Baba myself, but people these days are sensitive, foreigners especially. First, apparently, there was a mystified hush, then murmurings, and discussion, and next a great commotion, during which the interpreter escaped. Terry departed shortly after, leaving behind him a room strewn with dead men's effects and the photographers wailing and keening. Pity, because in fact Terry Sutton isn't particularly racist, or he hadn't been before trying to question the conclave in Queen's Gate. I've never heard him being racist about anyone except the Welsh. "Welsh goats," he calls them. That's because he plays forward for the Metropolitan Police and the Welsh sides are always walloping us.

So he got nothing out of the relatives except complaints about stolen money and the repercussions. He told me he hadn't been keen to hang on in the flat because among these unspecified repercussions there might've been one which took him hostage against the return of the shekels. Fairly sibylline, you'll agree, in view of what happened in Tehran not so long after. The American diplomats, the Shah's fortune, all that.

Not that the sum the defunct four had been toting around compared with what the Shah had salted away. The final guess at what the Pithley four were carrying, and even today it's still a guess, were a mere million.

We did what we could for the Somerest lads. There were leads apart from Queen's Gate. The car-hire firm for one.

The limousine which'd gone over the cliff had been hired to a Mr. Wallace Black of somewhere in Knightsbridge like Waylow Crescent, which didn't exist. Mr. Black had paid with a stolen credit card, and he wasn't Mr. Black.

The real Mr. Black was a tycoon and workaholic in Edgbaston who hadn't left his factory in forty years except to go home to sleep.

The car-hire manager described the unreal Mr. Black as big, shiny, and, far as I recall, "your typical con artist," which is the half-baked hindsight you hear all the time in this job. Whatever a typical con artist looks like, if this geezer'd looked like one, what was the manager doing renting him a car? Not just any car either, but a palace on wheels?

Still, the big and shiny checked out. Was he the big and shiny tout who'd been drumming up custom among tourists of a religious bent? Yes, pretty certainly he was, as it turned out, though we didn't know it then.

Terry didn't have to slog for this. We got it from the newspapers and only had to confirm it. Fleet Street got it from Peter Ramsden, the reporter down in Eastleigh. Ramsden had been on the blower saying there hadn't been four blokes in the car, there'd been five, or there had when it'd left Eastleigh. And the fifth wasn't an Arab, he was English, a chauffeur, and if he wasn't English he still wasn't an Arab, he was white Caucasian, and where was he?

This sort of information ought to be given to the police first, but it isn't where the press are involved, or not often. We're used to it, and it can work in our favour. For an ambitious hack like Ramsden, out in the sticks, this was a scoop. He made a hash of it for himself because he called the wrong paper. I think it was *The Guardian*. They'd have found the story unedifying. Same with *The Times*, who told him to tell the police. In desperation, I imagine, he started on the tabloids, where he should've gone in the first place. They shifted all right.

Suited us. Saved us the legwork. The press came down in an avalanche, which must've delighted the Berkeley, Claridges, the Savoy, the Ritz, Grosvenor House, Inn on the Park, all the top squats, because in five minutes the whisper was out there'd been a religious salesman haunting them, the five-star hotels, doing the rounds, offering the clientele his services as guide and driver.

The consensus among staff who'd been aware of him was that he was big, bland, and bluff, but discreet withal. He worked the bars and lounges, offering visits to cathedrals. He probably offered Jews synagogues, and Arabs mosques. We don't know, we never found him. Terry corralled a half-dozen assistants on to it for a while but we never discovered anything the press hadn't published, which amounted to approximately zero. Lots of supposition and creative thinking. He might've been American or Canadian. A barman at the Ritz swore he was South African.

Terry wanted to go to Eastleigh to talk to the reporter, Ramsden. He'd just traded in his jalopy for a terrifying custom-built job with streaks painted all over, and what he really wanted was to see if it'd open up on the motorway, with the Factory paying for the petrol. I told him no. The Somerset police had got from Ramsden all he knew, which was, "Sorry, John," chauffeuring gear, blue eyes, a shove which sent our young scribe tit over bum on the promenade, and a tooth. Top left incisor. That's an example of the sort of lead which promises well but fizzles out. Dentists, doctors, clinics—nothing.

Nothing from records on a specialist in sweeping God-fearing millionaires off on tours of hallowed sights, lifting their wallets, then disposing of them over cliffs. We'd only the reporter's word there was a chauffeur. Ramsden might've been overimaginative. He might've picked up the tooth from the ringside while covering the Eastleigh Boy's Brigade boxing finals. The Berkeley knew no more about the Arab foursome swanning off to the west country than the aunts and uncles had.

Dead end. The corpses and retinue were back in the Gulf. Somerset grafted on without results. Our bit of the file went on the shelf. Ramsden graduated with his portable Olivetti to London, where he was lost sight of. I had a poem in *Encounter*, of all places—my Marxist metaphysical phase.

> Where the spiritous confabs
> Of Oxonians and Cantabs
> Apropos unerring Arabs

Bidding for inflated scarabs
In New Bond Street's auction halls—
Blow the mind and crush the balls.

All I remember. Must've meant something at the time.
Got a tenner for it anyway. Couldn't decide whether to
sink the cheque in a litre of Glenlivet, or have it mounted.
Suppose it went into the housekeeping.

Ramsden's here in hospital, is he? He'll pull through.
Born lucky, that bugger.

Pity he didn't stay in Eastleigh all the same. He'd not
have walked into his chauffeur again if he'd kept clear of
Fleet Street. And both of us, we'd not be dead in this
forsaken, benighted Little Rock.

Pamela, *liebling*, I don't mean it. It's a great place,
truly, the greatest, the little I've seen of it.

Okay if I sleep a bit?

THREE

In gloomy moments, I see my newspaper career as having been downhill all the way, endlessly freewheeling. Fortunately, I have a well-developed sense of humour which has kept me buoyant, and sufficiently detached to see the Fleet Street rat race "steadily and whole," to borrow from Matthew Arnold. The snag to the freewheeling image, of course, is that to go downhill you have to have been reasonably elevated to start with. The Eastleigh *Examiner* may have suited Eastleigh, but it was never enough of a challenge to one of my potential.

My fifth-man scoop delivered me out of Eastleigh and into Fleet Street. It did no more than that because in less than a week the story was cold. Guilty or innocent, the chauffeur was never traced. If you've just received four sheiks of a million quid and deposited them in the sea—which was my guess—you're not going to wait around. By the time the police were sorting through the bodies on the rocks he'd have been on his way to Hong Kong, or Cape Town, or Mexico. Little Rock even.

I'm getting ahead of myself.

Nothing I could do was going to keep the story warm. In fiction no doubt I'd have spurted off on the trail with my notebook and ball-point, but if the combined sleuths of Fleet Street and Scotland Yard were failing to find him, Peter Ramsden working alone probably wasn't going to manage it. In fact, no one suggested I try. I didn't want to find him anyway.

I'd have been happy if he'd been found. Nobody wants

a maniac running loose. But I didn't want to do the finding. More than likely he wouldn't have remembered me, not from that one brief pavement encounter in bucketing rain. But if he had? He might've responded ungently to a potential witness for the prosecution asking him his life's story.

The scoop was my last as well as my first. I still think if there'd been an opening on *The Guardian*, or any of the quality papers, I'd have prospered. Not in terms of scoops. They're rare enough. Not financially either because the money's better on the pops, though God knows where it goes. But I wasn't ecstatic on the popular press, even at the beginning. Especially at the beginning. And I can't say things have improved much. I'd have taken a salary cut and lived in Wapping with a gas ring and a shared bog down the corridor if I could've shunted to worthwhile stuff on a class paper.

Would I? To start with perhaps I would have. I've never had money, not real money, and being a newspaperman can give you a taste for it because you meet all sorts, including the very rich. I've met Sir James Goldsmith, and Nancy Reagan when she came over for the royal wedding, and Elton John, and I'd like what they've got. Obviously, my salary on the *Post* isn't in the same league, but it could be a great deal worse, and the trouble with a comfy standard of living is that you get to wear it like a bandage over a sore spot, so that if any of it's peeled off—ouch.

Perhaps now it'll happen without any drop in salary, a class paper, now *I'm* news, not simply writing it. I assume I'm news anyway. *The Times?* Theatre, think pieces, a quality gossip column for and about the people who count. Prestige and style and a place in society.

From Eastleigh I joined the *Express*. A mistake for both of us. After three months and some serious chats in the pub with the news editor I moved to the *Sun*, which proved a worse mistake. In nearly seven years in Fleet Street I've been with four papers. Not a record, but they're getting to know me, which in itself is surprising because I don't stand out as a demon, door-stepping, button-holing newshound, inventing quotes for old ladies and trying to bribe Buckingham Palace butlers for the latest on the royals.

It boils down to compatibility. Like marriage, I imagine. My jobs haven't been marriages, they've been affairs, where it doesn't matter if you're compatible or not because by definition, as an affair, it's going to end, you know you'll be moving on. I discovered in Fleet Street I was hypersensitive. Reporting for the Eastleigh *Examiner* had never been like reporting for the national tabloids.

On the late shift, when the first editions came in and the *Mirror*'s front page might splash a duchess's only daughter being raped and beheaded by a Grenadier guardsman, which we'd missed, the news desk would be thrown into a terrible state, moanings and recriminations, and if no one livelier were available, I'd be shot out to check with the duchess. Or with the guardsman.

I'd get to the address at one in the morning, watch the house and its lighted windows for a while from across the street, then phone the news desk and tell them, "No answer, sorry, they must've cleared off, shall I come back or hang on?"

Let's be honest, I'd no objection to reading such stories, or writing them. It was asking the duchess for the details at one in the morning that I wasn't brilliant at. I still can't do it. On the *Examiner* there'd been none of this, and there's very little on the posh papers, but to be happy with the pops you have to be able to talk your way inside, pocket the daughter's photograph from off the piano, and enjoy it. Often these methods are disgusting, but there's a load of holier-than-thou hypocrisy talked about it. You hear these hotshot reporters and photographers called scum by the same people who want all the details for their breakfast reading plus the picture.

Still, plenty of jobs were not nosing into people's misery, or risking a punch on the nose from some beer-bellied leader during a dock strike. The job which led to the horror of the last ten days looked easy, instructive, entertaining, and right up Peter Ramsden's alley.

*   *   *

"Peter, if anyone needs being born again it's probably you," my news editor said, handing over a gaudy press kit in the form of a plastic briefcase filled with giveaway pens, notepads, and bumf.

Helen Goodenough is my first woman news editor. She's done it all, including in her salad days the Algerian war and Vietnam. Also behind her are three husbands and several thousand hectolitres of gin. Plenty more in front of her, too, I wouldn't be surprised, if her liver doesn't bring her down.

We arrived more or less simultaneously on the *Post* when it started up in May. Not started up, strictly. Merged rather, changed its name and proprietor in the latest upheaval, take-over and in-fighting in the Street of Adventure. I'd been two years with the *Mail* and probably should've stayed, because they had plenty to get your teeth into, but opportunities on the *Post* looked rosier, and I was offered more money. We're a tabloid, and we have our daily nude, but it's still in the balance how popular we're going to be.

The time would've been about seven when Helen beckoned me over. This was two weeks ago, nearly. You could tell she'd finished for the day because she was heaving herself into her sable preparatory to the White Swan. Before leaving she usually allots whatever jobs there might be for the next day.

I was on the three-to-ten shift, and idle, waiting for the Thames to flood, or the Houses of Parliament to burst into flames. On the three-to-ten shift you're idle until five minutes to ten when something breaks that keeps you going until three next morning. The briefcase she passed me smelled of metal polish and was stamped with a representation of Christ crucified, gold rods radiating from his head, and the message in gold:

Be Born Again in Jesus Christ
Christ in Britain—Britain in Christ
Great Awakening Campaign
The Reverend Pastor Jody C. James

Minister & Founder, First Born-Again Church of God
Little Rock, Arkansas
With the Born-Again Gospel Singers

I looked in the diary at the next day's engagements.
There he was, Peter Ramsden, down for Jody C. James,
6:30 P.M., Princess Hall. Maggie Wells had the headmis-
tress's conference, to which she was welcome. Ross Car-
ter, our compulsory Aussie from Dingbat Creek, had a
Foyle's lunch where the guest of honour was to be one of
our venerable knighted actors.

"Couldn't I swap with Ross?" I asked Helen. "Bible
bashing, evangelism—just the thing for colonials. Ross is
very basic."

"Ross is in need of culture, darling, not religion. Anyway, he's a Jew, isn't he? These born-again people sound
like an offshoot of the Ku Klux Klan. They'd never let in
anyone who's circumcised."

She gave me an inquiring look.

"None of your business," I said.

"Peter, would I pry?" She was checking the ingredients
of her handbag. "Don't forget, while you're there, a small
prayer for me and the *Post,* please. I've already been on
two papers which folded."

With which discouraging valediction she sabled out; a
swathed, squat figure, antennae quivering towards gin.
The reason she didn't swap Ross's and my jobs was
because she'd have had to have altered the diary and
recovered the press kit, which would've cut into her gin
time by twenty seconds.

Also, because I didn't push it. I wasn't averse to looking in on the born-again lot. The fact is I freak out over
gospel singing. Mahalia Jackson. All those authentic, ethnic, writhing, hand-clapping, yea-shouting, blood-churning
hallelujahs. Snakes and faith healing. Faulkner country.
Hey-yeeeaaah!

In small doses anyway. A not totally disabling fix of
explosive black Mississippi—or Little Rock, in this instance, going by the message on the briefcase. You don't
get to see and hear much hot gospelling in London.

*   *   *

My expectations were out, and Helen's by and large were correct. Almost the only aspect of the First Born-Again Church of God which was black was the audience, or some of it. A quarter of them were middle-aged and elderly West Indians. Much of the gospel singing, though not all, was more syrupy than hot.

Without checking, I wouldn't have cared to hint that they were the Ku Klux Klan, with Jody James as Vizier Grand Dragon. Newspaper history shows that such hinting is booby-trapped with libel suits. But they well might've been, they were reactionary enough, the press kit offering clues galore. I opened it on the tube heading south for Stockwell and the Princess Hall. An envelope fell to the floor. "Your Contribution to the First Born-Again Church of God—The Lord Blesses the Gift and the Giver."

Almost entirely the loose pages were concerned with the *curriculum vitae* of three people: God, Jesus, and the Reverend Jody C. James, who had got it all together and was offering salvation through the true word granted in a vision to himself while planing hickory wood in his humble workshop behind his house in Little Rock. What the word was he wasn't saying in the press release. Whatever it was, I'd have bet you'd have had to pay money for it.

I surmised there'd not be much change left in your pocket either after a visit to Creation World. This multimillion-dollar complex still under construction outside Little Rock, as illustrated in a brochure of breathtaking vulgarity, looked to be a kind of spiritual fun fair. There was the church itself, gardens, shopping arcades, a restaurant, indoor and outdoor pools, and a born-again baptism pool. There was a scale replica of the Reverend James's carpenter's shop where the word had been revealed to him. There were two Halls of Fame—Old and New Testaments—a Genesis City ("See the Creation Unfold Before Your Eyes"), a Garden of Eden ("Children Under 13 Not Admitted"), and a Hall of Evolution depicted by a photo of the building's exterior only and carrying the caption "Visit Our Famed Hall of Evolution: The Lord Has a Special Blessing for Those Who Enjoy a Joke."

The Hall of Evolution was probably an empty room with the joke on the paying customer. For thirty dollars there were vouchers offering sensational reductions.

Apologies if I sound sour. I'm ninety per cent atheist. The uncommitted ten per cent is at the disposal of anyone who cares to try and convince me, and I don't mean this as a challenge. I'd be happy to believe, but I'm still to be convinced that the intellect can do anything about it. So you're thrown back on grace, innocence, or whatever, which you have or you haven't.

If I'm sour it's really nothing to do with religion anyway, it's politics masquerading as religion, this born-again church's politics especially. From the clues in the press release, together with what I was to gather later from listening to the Reverend James, he was for God, America, the family, Bible reading, prayer in schools, proselytising, and massive spending on nuclear missiles and bombs.

He was against liberals, communists, feminists, queers, abortion, pornography, sex education in schools, euthanasia, welfare, red tape, and gun control.

Well, quite a few unborn-again voters would go along with several planks in that platform. It's using God as the glue and nails and varnish which gives me the ague. I'd be delighted to be indifferent, and certainly you can't separate religion and politics into hermetically sealed boxes, but it's criminal that these born-again dictators should con the housekeeping money out of mindless people by promising salvation, insinuating they alone have the answers, and playing on gut prejudices.

The press kit gave me more background on God and Jesus than on Mr. James, for whom I thought there was surprisingly little. Plenty on his revelation in his workshop, on starting his church, his achievement building membership to a hundred thousand in five years, and his weekly coast-to-coast television hour, "The Born-Again Gospel Show." But none of the personal touches which give a story human interest, not even a word on whether he was married, and virtually nothing on his early life.

Why not? He'd have had to invent, and invention can be investigated?

I'd not be investigating him. If there'd been anything worth investigating the American press would've been onto it, probably the Washington *Post* leading the charge. In any case, he was in Britain for only a week. Tonight the opening, day after tomorrow Glasgow, then Manchester—run for cover, Mancunians!— and back to London for a final hoedown at the Albert Hall, before returning to the U.S.A. next Sunday.

Am I anticipating, or did I really sense from this skimming of the handouts that there might be something unsavoury about the Reverend? Certainly by the time the tube reached Stockwell I'd developed a distaste. All that was going to save the evening would be the hottest of hot gospelling from the choir.

That a disgruntled Jew, Catholic, evolutionist—no matter who—should arrive with scatter guns and blow away the whole holy parcel of them, and thus a story for the morrow, was too much to hope for.

I arrived late but I'd missed nothing. On sale in the entrance were born-again key rings, T-shirts, literature, and at a pricey six pounds each, long-playing records by BAGS, an acronym which served both show and singers impartially. The auditorium was packed, which at least warmed it up a bit. There'd been ice on the pavement outside. The temperature of the Princess Hall depends on body warmth and cigarette smoke. The slogan on the T-shirt worn over layers of jerseys by a lady fundamentalist in the front row read, "Rock of Ages—Not Ages of Rocks."

In front of her, against the stage, two tables and a dozen chairs had been set aside for the press. Half the chairs were empty. No sign of television cameras. Perhaps the media were saving themselves for the final shindig at the Albert Hall. Perhaps they just weren't thrilled. Names make news, and the name Jody James was unfamiliar in Britain, though admittedly the hall was crowded. Either they were here for the singing or the computer staff had got hold of mailing lists.

For Billy Graham there'd have been automatic cover-

age, if only a paragraph, even after thirty years and his
message unchanged. Timelessness may be what spiritual
messages are about, but journalism deals in timeliness, and
names.

I sat beside Isobel Wood from *The Times.* In the first
place she has shorthand, not that it was likely to be needed
tonight. Secondly, I was once in love with her, though
nothing came of it. It might have, because I'm fairly sure
she fancied me, perhaps still does, but she's the kind
who's afraid of her emotions. Anyway, she's married
now.

"Brought your prayer mat?" she said.

"I'm not here to pray, I'm here to sing. Gimmee that
ol'-time religion."

"Optimist. Listen to it."

To one side of a stage hung with flags, gold and silver
drapes, and a banner proclaiming "Great Awakening Campaign," an old-fashioned youth wearing a crew cut and a
monogrammed scarlet silk angel robe was seated at an
electronic organ, sicklily playing a dirge. Mainly he stayed
with the high notes, which strained and oozed out of the
amplifiers like toothpaste. No one else was onstage, which
was bare apart from a table swathed in more gold and
silver, and which bore a lectern, microphone, decanter of
water, and a glass. Gold and silver curtains and massed
Union Jacks and Stars and Stripes hung at the back of the
stage, where low platforms had been placed in an arc,
perhaps for the gospel singers.

I say gold and silver. It may have been paint. I don't
know what it was, other than theatrical and in dismal taste.
Since America's religious establishments pull in twenty
billion dollars a year, so I've discovered, and this one
presumably had its share, probably it was gold and silver.
Insured by Lloyds.

The audience was expectant and decently hushed, cough-
ing from winter colds, chattering only in whispers, and
flipping through souvenir booklets bought from the stewards patrolling the aisles. These stewards in scarlet jackets
were male and female, fit and smiling, like cabin crew on
a jetliner. The organ electronically mewled.

"Don't be misled, it'll end up an orgy of hallelujahs," I said.

"It'll end up a riot," said Dizzy. "Denis Fortune's in the third row from the back, with his team."

I stood up to see. Denis Fortune is South London's gay rights' champion. Neatly bearded, hair short at the sides, and Calvin Klein jeans. Scuffles have a way of breaking out whenever he finagles entrance into right-wing rallies where the call goes out for draconian penalties against homosexuals, criminals, foreigners, the unemployed, and women. Before I was able to spot him the house lights dimmed, then went out.

I sat down. The stage brightened. The organ struck a martial air which was almost but not quite "Onward Christian Soldiers." From left and right there filed onstage two crocodiles of scrubbed young men and women wearing scarlet angel robes identical to the organist's. There were a score of them, including one black. BAGS, the Born-Again Gospel Singers, I assumed. With but one black, *adios* to hopes of hallelujahs.

The choir took up its position on the platform at the rear of the stage and broke into song.

> "Born again for Jesus!
> Born again for God!
> Turned around for glory
> Like the farmer turns the sod . . ."

The tune was derivative and the words fairly extraordinary, but the sound was stirring. A harmonious, full-throated blend of rock, ragtime, and Welsh chapel. No question, they could sing. There was a lead singer, a syncopated *bel canto* tenor, who carried the refrain, while the choir wah-wahed and belted in with responses. Even without mikes the joyful noise would've soared above the uncertain sing-along noises from the audience.

> "Born again!
> Born again!
> Fight for the right

            To be men—
            Born again!''

    The final, climactic ''Born again!'' was not so much sung as shouted. I half expected a leap and a punching of the air, as from cheerleaders. They stood in a scarlet arc graded by height, two six-footers in the centre, but rising to six foot six at the extremities. The one who caught my eye was a bony redhead a little off centre. Her red hair was frizzed and her facial bones were pronounced enough to have been pounced on by an anatomy lecturer the day the demonstration skull went missing. The other girls had that fetching but sanitized and ultimately boring college sophomore bloom. All worth a detour, I'm not saying I'd have rejected advances from any of them. After all, competition for a place in the choir must've been tough, and once you break down a hundred thousand membership, hiving off the grannies, infants, tone-deaf, and plain uglies, you're still going to be left with the pick of not a few presentable songsters. Not being out of the sun-kissed sophomore mould, the bony redhead must've had other qualifications. Certainly she sang with gusto. Perhaps Daddy had contributed over the odds to the BAGS exchequer.

    Perhaps she was particularly barmy about God. She'd have made a smashing singing helpmeet for any revivalist banjoist.

    Verse two was about being born again for Christ, and turned around and sanctified, like bread of heaven sliced. Dizzy and I exchanged glances. Now they had the hang of the tune the audience sang along with verve, and when the hymn ended with a last, clamorous ''Born again!'' they applauded, then sat back coughing and recovering their breath. The stage lights dimmed and the choir started a doleful humming. A spotlight lit a circle of stage into which, out from the wings, walked a big fellow in a dark three-piece suit carrying a Bible. Applause erupted anew, and self-conscious whoopings from the groundlings.

    The spotlight illumined the man's progress across the stage to the side of the table where he stood facing the audience and holding aloft the Bible. Mounting applause from the congregation. A crescendo of humming from the scarlet arc. The spotlight evaporated in the brightening yellow light of the stage.

"The electrician's working well," I said.

"You didn't sing a note," said Dizzy. "You said you were here to sing."

"I'll sing when Jody sings. Is this him?"

Dizzy turned to the Press Association reporter on her left, who turned to Ruth Butterworth from the *Telegraph* on his left. The humming and applause had ceased and the big man had lowered his Bible and was beaming at the audience when Dizzy, having received the answer, turned back to me. She whispered, "Probably."

"My dear, good friends, I bring greetings from the First Born-Again Church of God," the man with the Bible boomed into the microphone. "Greetings, friendship, and Christian love from our church, from the United States of America, and from our own blessed Land of Opportunity."

He paused, smiling, and gesturing with his Bible as if in anticipation of, and already calming, an engulfing applause. Such applause as there was came from uncertain hand-clappers and one or two un-English whoopers—the whoops, I suspected, were from the red-jacketed stewards. Later, I learned that Land of Opportunity was the official nickname for Arkansas, but since no one else in the audience could've been aware of this either, and were hardly to be expected to get excited about Arkansas if they had, the reference fell flat.

"Jesus told Nicodemus, 'Except a man be born again, he cannot see the kingdom of God.' " The man had closed his eyes. He held his Bible two-handed to his chest. "And the Lord said, 'How long halt ye between two opinions?' Shall we stand?"

The audience stood, the press remained seated. Far from rabble-rousing, the man's tone was low-key. He didn't gesture, apart from an occasional hoick of his Bible. He was on intimate terms with God, his voice was sonorous and southern, with imperfect "r's," which didn't appear to bother him, and his text, these two opinions we were halting between, they were not, or at any rate not so far,

capitalism or communism, black power or white supremacy, or the marriage bond versus adultery, but nothing
more exceptional than right and wrong. He was another
six-footer, fortyish, with the bland, pudding face of an
overfed baby. His double-breasted suit helped to conceal
what were probably too many kilos, and though I couldn't
clearly see his eyes from the press table, he was familiar.
His concession to the overall colour scheme on stage was a
scarlet tie.

Dizzy was writing. That's the difference between *The
Times* and us, because there was no story here for the
Post. Frankly, I couldn't imagine *The Times* either, for all
its acres of space, being knocked out by this rambling
monologue in support of virtue. Dizzy slid her notebook in
my direction. She'd written, *Ruth says "How long halt ye
etc" not t Lord but Elijah.*

Underneath, I wrote, *Ruth shd be on a quiz show.*

Dizzy had started to pen some facetiousness in reply
when the prayer ended, a chord mewled from the organ,
and the man took a step forward. He welcomed us as his
sheep, and at last introduced himself as shepherd and
pastor, our friend, the Reverend Jody C. James. He delivered a homily on Jesus being similarly friendly to all who
made a friend of him, then retired stage left and stood with
his Bible clasped to his bosom while the choir sang
a bouncy number about "Counting on the Man at the
Wheel."

> "Count, count, count
> On the Man at the Wheel,
> Tell him your troubles,
> Tell him how you feel . . ."

Banal, the Reverend and his junket, though a drama
critic might have felt obliged to add that all was profes-
sionally staged and costumed, and the audience seemed
riveted. At the press table we began to doze while Jody
James talked about love in the intimate sitting-room style
which, I suppose, had won him his coast-to-coast television audience. Even when his points became controversial,

and his language weighted, his tone remained calm. Ingratiating, you could have said.

". . . those slayers of unborn life, those tormented assassins of innocence . . ."

Dizzy stirred and poised her Biro.

"I could tell you, friends, of evils unimaginable. I could tell of fleshly lusts, drug abuse, and illicit sexual passion. Of sin which causes our Lord Jesus to bleed and suffer once more."

But he did not tell, although in a sense he already had. He aimed a beringed finger at the organist, as if there sat the perpetrator of the evils unimaginable. Then he stepped aside, hugging his Bible. The organ oozed and the gospel singers were off again, crooning about redemption, while the stoked passions and neuroses of the congregation were left to steam unassuaged.

Next he talked about the creation, Adam and Eve, and money. The stewards passed round gaping red plastic buckets for contributions. During this rite the organ whined and the Reverend expounded his theory of what he called cash-flow circularism, whereby the more one donated, the more the Lord in his wisdom would bless the donor with higher profits in his business enterprises, salary increases, and insights into ways of reducing taxation levels. I'd have called it a holy rip-off.

"Stand up," he called out, "all those who pledge a hundred dollars—no, hold it right there! I've goofed!" He hadn't goofed at all, he'd been rehearsing this for weeks. "I mean a hundred pounds!"

In the intermission Dizzy and I fled to the Trafalgar for a dram.

Dizzy said, "There's nought, no doubt, so much the spirit calms as rum"—rum wasn't what she was drinking, she was drinking bitter—"and true religion."

After the intermission, the Reverend finally told us. In a prayer, his voice soft and southern, his eyes closed, from stage centre.

". . . shore up for us the family circle, O God. Cement the wall against all adulterers, abortionists, and black perverts as the bricklayers of old cemented the walls of Gath and Hebron, or Jericho itself when the bugles blew . . . .''

This, in my view, was Anthony at Caesar's funeral, playing on emotions, crescendo and diminuendo, building then breaking off. From his first chatty confidences, I realised, he had been building. At any moment he'd be breaking off again, bringing in the singers, leaving us tumescent and unappeased. His treacly drawl was hypnotic.

''. . . that you raise high the stockade against the princes of darkness, the misguided minions of communism, the alley rapists and muggers with their social security cheques—''

''Lord!'' someone in the audience said.

''. . . the homosexuals and sexually tormented, the idlers who live off our backs, whether in my own country or here in your fine, old-world London, England, paying not a cent in taxes like you and me, friends, but squandering their spiritual inheritance and welfare cheques in disco halls, massage parlours—''

''Fascist!''

''—where the whores of the perverted black anti-Christ—''

''Pig chauvinist! Nazi!''

''This is it,'' Dizzy said, standing for a better view of the audience.

Ruth, from the *Telegraph,* who's five foot two or three, climbed up on her chair. At the back of the hall the struggling was confused, as always with such demonstrations. Scarlet-jacketed stewards converged, chairs toppled and were lifted as weapons, banners unfurled from under anoraks. ''Gay Rights.'' ''Keep Your Morality Off Our Backs.'' ''Abort Racism Not Peace.'' ''Freedom To Choose.'' I glimpsed Denis Fortune, bearded and skinny, wrestling with a scarlet battery of stewards. A bosomy feminist was laying about her with a rolled newspaper which, judging from the results, concealed lead piping. Onstage the Reverend Jody C. James stood with his Bible raised, mouthing inaudibly. Any moment now the coppers would be in.

Or not. I've never known chapter and verse of the law about public meetings, but having covered a few hundred I know the police are never on view. The uniformed police, that's to say. Special Branch characters in trench coats may be lurking. The helmeted lot are outside, and if someone nips out to complain about skulls being broken, in they come.

Coppers or no coppers, we had a story. Nothing earth-moving, but breakfast entertainment for everyone, and everyone happy. I didn't have the second scoop of my career because I was only seventy per cent sure that the Reverend Jody James was my long-ago chauffeur from the Eastleigh esplanade.

Libel awards being what they are, in this business you have to be a hundred per cent sure, pretty well.

FOUR

Don't ask me how I got embroiled with the God-botherers. Damned if I know.

Pamela, light of my life (*recorded P.O. Kremer, pausing to shift her chair six inches back, out of reach of the patient's wandering hand*). It's not true. Delete expletive and all the rest. Start again. Randy? I mean, ready?

We'll start in the pub, The Feathers, off Ebury Street, as good a place as any. Saturday before last, lunchtime. I was having a reviving few before packing it in for the day because I'd spent the last three days and all morning with this crowd from Bahawalpur, fourteen of them, all related, trying to convince them that unless they came up with something such as a reason, or better still a piece of paper, ideally with Her Majesty's signature, they were going to be shipped back to Bahawalpur before their biriani was cold.

I hadn't asked to be moved to Illegal Immigration but I didn't protest. It made a change. Who knew, there might turn up the odd, mad maharani slipping you a ruby for stamping her permit? They're not all pitiful Pakistanis and hopeful Jamaicans either, the ones we have to send back. We had this bloke with the lizard-skin shoes and Italian name from Las Vegas, no heartbreak sending him back. But mostly they're a mournful lot you can't help doing your best for, short of forgery, or sneaking them in through a side entrance. What's another handful? In my corner of Islington there'd still be no milk or tinned papayas on Sundays if it weren't for Mr. and Mrs. Sayeed at their

Good Food Emporium, even though they do charge you.
The commander'd had me in more than once to let me
know he agreed, everyone agreed, no one had anything but
sympathy for these people, but our job was enforcing the
law as it stood, not twisting it like a paper clip, and if I
wanted it changed why didn't I resign and stand for Parliament? I've been only ten weeks with the Illegal Immigration Squad. Another ten weeks, they'll have had enough of
me, I'll be shunted to dog handling. Naming the puppies.
If I live. God knows it's all different now.

So. I was in The Feathers with Terry Sutton, who's with
Forgery these days. He says they've got an index of over
three hundred different banknotes and after you've studied
thirty the figures and colours start to blur, and they all look
the same, like Chinamen. Anyway, he was reading the
paper. He's not much of a chatter until he's read the sports
pages six times, but he must've finished with the sports
and progressed to the domestic front because he said,
"Denis Fortune's been living it up again. Twelve arrests at
the Princess Hall. BAGS."

"Bags? Feminists?"

"It's a show, they're evangelists, the Born-Again Gospel Show, over from the States," explained Terry Sutton,
reading. "Like the Palladium with hymns. They believe
God created the world in seven days."

"Six. 'And he rested on the seventh day.' "

"The Reverend Jody C. James. Heard of him?"

"No."

" 'By Peter Ramsden, Our Own Reporter.' We've heard
of *him*."

"You may have."

"When we were in Vice. Right? The one who saw the
chauffeur nobody else saw. The Arabs who went over the
cliff."

"That's going back a bit. Read me the Quik-n-Eezy
recipe. And drink up, lad. The other half and I'm off."

That was the beginning, and that was all, or it should've
been all. Far as my starring role goes it would've been all
too, evangelists not being the concern of Illegal Immigration. But for Miriam.

* * *

She was on the sitting-room sofa looking like some sort of smashing contemporary madonna with one breast bared and Sam belching and floundering on her lap. A head on the TV screen was chuntering about a steel toe cap for Christmas, for gardeners, a contraption you strapped over the toes to stop them being lopped off by the lawnmower.

"All right if I switch it off?" I said.

"No. I want to talk to you. I think you ought to do something about these born-again people." She might've looked more like a madonna had both breasts been bare, or covered, but the rumpled effect was more exotic than spiritual. "You can take him if you like. I think he's had enough."

We became parents later than the average and the upheaval's been fairly dramatic, but Miriam's always threatening a second. I held Sam by the ankles and swung him upside down. That's his idea of paradise. Miriam gets anxious but she can't say anything because she read in a book how it stiffens the sinews and summons up the blood. I tried it on Miriam once and she bit my ankle.

I sat down with him. "Who da great-a-beeg cheese, hey?" Papadom makes overripe fruit of us all. "Who da beeg cheese round here these days?"

"Stop bouncing him, you'll have it all over you. Listen. You should've seen this preacher, James somebody. I'm serious. Did you know in America they're burning books on evolution? Why wouldn't it spread here? Well, why wouldn't it?"

From the screen came a metallic screech. The programme presenter in steel toe caps had put his feet into an electric lawnmower. Sparks showered.

"It's the effects department," I said. "In fact, those blades are rubber. Why aren't we watching the wrestling? Whaddya say, Sam, Sam, dirty old man? Is afternoon telly da pitty-pitty-pits or ain't it?"

"Heaven's sake, turn it off. You just missed this born-again preacher. Honestly, why should they be allowed to get away with it? He tied the interviewer in knots, some futile girl, at least they might've found someone who'd heard of Darwin. There's a piece about him in *The Guardian*. Anyone who argues gets beaten up. There were scores of arrests last night.''

"Twelve.''

"Wait and see. He's against divorce, abortion, evolution, rock music, he's obviously against women, he'll be against blacks, Jews, queers, and Catholics, but of course the interviewer never asked. He's got this smile and Swannee River voice, and he carries God around with him like a credit card. It's sickening and I say you should do something about it.''

I suppose most of us these days, in England, are what you might call freethinkers. All right, nonthinkers. Miriam's one of the minority who don't call themselves that, or anything, and I'd describe her as a worried Christian. Not all that worried, but enough to take any joy out of it. She'd like to believe, and my guess is she does, most of the time. She says the real barrier to believing is wanting to be certain, because there can't be certainty. That's the one thing she's certain about. You shouldn't expect certainty, she said, and if you don't, if you're not chasing after irrefutable proofs, it's perfectly reasonable to believe because logic doesn't make nonsense of God, neither does science, and the reasons for believing are good, starting with the scripture as witness.

We don't disagree on too much, but we don't often delve into the eternal verities, first causes, all that. We should, it's my fault we don't, total failure of the imagination, but it's also that I get muddled, which starts me shouting, or at any rate raising my voice, when likely she hasn't even said anything. I remember shouting at her once that I didn't have time for a spiritual quest, and at that moment the eternal verities were the baby having a cold, and how much forelock touching was going to get the promotion and pay rise to cover the extra fourpence on a pint of milk? So I tend to avoid the big themes, and Miriam does too, because she's not thrilled about being shouted at, though she's capable of shouting back or, far more petrifying, assuming that voice like rustling ice cubes.

So her being worked up against this born-again bloke

was unusual. I was inclined to write it off to afternoon telly. I've seen afternoon telly. It's so wet you want the tumbler-dryer alongside to put your head in. The odd thing was, Miriam's got her feet on the ground. She doesn't get heated about a parcel of visiting evangelists.

"I'll look into it." I said.

"I'm sorry." She wasn't in the least sorry. "I'm telling you, I'm serious. What about Sam? What sort of life's he going to have if fanatics like this crowd get away with it? They've got millions of supporters already in the States, and more every day, and now they're here. What if this James creature becomes the next President? The world was not created in six days. That's a lie. It's as simple as that. You're Illegal Immigration. Why did you let them in?"

"They're not illegal immigrants."

"Not the point at all."

"Beg pardon, thought you were making it the point. They didn't come in with guns, drugs, or plague either, and you can't keep people out because they think the world was made in six days, or it's flat, or it's going to end next Wednesday. All right? If those are your reasons for keeping them out you're no better than they are."

That did it. Having said we don't often disagree, I can reveal that this was an occasion when we did. Except at bottom we didn't, because Miriam isn't really for beating the crazies to a paste. If they're that crazy, I argued, they should be encouraged to tell it from the rooftops. More rope you gave them, quicker they'd hang themselves. You had to leave it to the horse sense of ordinary people. Truth would out.

Miriam argued that truth wouldn't necessarily do anything of the kind. I hadn't the foggiest idea what was going on, she said. I probably thought disillusioned youth was still America's most vocal group, but I was ten years out of date. Moral issues were what counted now. Why didn't I get off my backside and go and hear what this Jody James had to say? The activists today were right-wing, born-again evangelicals. They were biblical inerrant militants. God knows where she got her language from. I think she was saying biblical inerrant militants were people who'd clock anyone who suggested the Bible might err from the literal truth. She said it was terrifying, more and more votes were going to the born-again right, at this rate the next President would be banning everything except reading Leviticus all day Sunday, and now they were exporting their illness to us. She wasn't having Sam growing up in a world which people believed God created in six days simply because it was written in a book which was strong in poetry and marvellous for metaphor, but thin on historical fact.

I told her she exaggerated. Sam was swimming his long-distance breaststroke across my chest. My tie was going to have to visit the cleaners because half of it was in his mouth. Miriam said I was a sloppy, liberal do-gooder, and I thanked her. The spat might have clattered on but she had to hurtle back to Knightsbridge and the Royal Archaeological Society where she's caterer producing lunch and supper for archaeologists with bits of broken pottery in their pockets. We've acquired an *au pair* to help with Sam, a cigarette-smoking Finn named Sigrid who should've been somewhere in the house, blowing smoke, but I wanted to hold the lad for a while yet, see what'd be next on the list when he'd finished eating my tie.

We both received a kiss from Miriam, Sam's as sloppy as my liberal sentiments, mine somewhat perfunctory.

She agreed, sighing, she'd exaggerated. It was just that she worried about Sam, and everyone young and impressionable, all the naïve and the disappointed who were looking for instant answers. Give these fundamentalists their week in Britain, she agreed, they'd vanish back to the States, an insubstantial pageant faded, leaving not a hosanna behind, not a dent in the fabric of society, just an indifferent memory, and, on the pavements outside the halls where they'd ranted, a scattering of antiabortion leaflets.

"No, no," I disagreed. "They're a pest. You're spot on as always. It's a question of where to draw the line." Sam had transferred his mouth from the tie to a shirt button. Threads of saliva glitteringly extended, broke, and swung. "Tomorrow. I'll make some inquiries."

* * *

We don't have a God Squad at the Yard. We've got Murder, Drugs, Forgery, Fraud, Post Office, Art and Antiques, Illegal Immigration—that's me. Sounds comprehensive when you start listing it. There's the Flying Squad, Regional Crime Squad, Criminal Intelligence, Stolen Motor Vehicles, Special Branch, Traffic, Mounted, Thames Division, Dogs, Communications, Community Relations. What've I missed? Where would you slot God into that lot?

Fact is, it wouldn't be difficult. Depends on the crime. If he arrived wearing a long white beard on a flight from the heavenly kingdom with no passport or work permit, and slipped through immigration, and later was found drawing unemployment benefits, he'd be my pigeon. After the usual questioning we might let him stay and we might not.

But there are grey areas and overlapping. Special Branch would be interested in God because they carry the can for VIPs. They don't always agree on who qualifies as a VIP, but God would. He'd qualify is what I mean. Judging from the initials, this Jody C. James might've considered himself the son of God, but Special Branch didn't because they'd provided no guard for him, and when I gave them a buzz they weren't gripped, though they said they had an eye on him, which I doubt. Special Branch like to think of themselves as all that stands between the country and invasion by ape-men with poisoned umbrellas, but you have to be a pretty well-documented threat to national security before they get their fingers out. Miriam in her antievangelist mood might've convinced them, just.

There's overlapping but there's still no one in the CID specialising in church matters. Guideline or parameterwise we are not overencumbered with church-related incidents. Next day, Sunday, back in the office, there wasn't too much to unearth on the Reverend James and his road show. Nothing from Records. From Intelligence, copies of the entry permit, unilluminating press clippings, a load of born-again handouts for the media, and the report from Division on the rumpus at the Princess Hall. A pretty innocuous affair that sounded too. Not to be breathed in the same breath with our race punch-ups, and when the young unemployed let off steam, or come to that some of the old Empire Loyalist barneys at the Caxton Hall in my uniform days.

Still, I tried. For Miriam and Sam. Frankly, I had the time. My efforts on behalf of the sorrowing troupe from Bahawalpur had gone to the Home Office and nothing much else was doing. November's slack in Illegal Immigration. Too cold is my guess. They're not stupid out in the old outposts of empire, they know their seasons, they're not going to float about for days in freezing fog looking for a beach if they can postpone until summer. The Bahawalpurans were the exception, either uniformed or impatient.

I gave my born-again inquiries an hour, which was stretching it because there was zero to inquire into. So everyone seemed to think anyway. If it hadn't been for Ramsden's antics, probably there'd never have been any inquiries after my two penn'orth. The BAGS touring company would've faded back to the States, and there'd have been not another peep from Miriam. One call I made, I'd hardly say it was an inquiry, was to Willie Smith, three hundred and fifty miles away in the frozen wastes.

"Willie? Henry. Could you leave off tossing your caber a moment? Are you sober?"

"Unfortunately. Don't tell me you're about to cross the border."

"Willie's a superintendent with Glasgow CID. I once gave him a crooked walking stick gift-wrapped in tartan ribbon. He sent me a jar of whelks from Harrods.

"Not unless I'm chained in a sack," I told him. "Hear you've got snow, apart from your usual problems, like a country full of Scots."

"What's on your mind, you limp Sassenach?"

"You've got some Yankee evangelists at your Kelvin Hall tonight. The First Born-Again Church of God. A preacher called Jody James."

"I'd heard. I hadn't thought of going. I'm a decently lapsed Catholic, but I'm not that lapsed."

"According to Miriam this joker's against everything

including half-lapsed Catholics. She saw him on the telly
and he's put the wind up her. We had them in London
three nights ago, there was a disagreement over whether
the world's flat."

"Canna ye find nothing better to fight about? Tell Miriam from me to stop worrying. Glasgow's the cradle of
disagreements. Has she not heard of Celtic and Rangers?
A punch-up releases tensions and resolves nothing, letting
us look forward to the next."

"All I'm doing is passing the word so I can report back.
I've promised I'll save Sam and the nation from evangelicals."

"Your nation's beyond saving, but for Sam and Miriam
I'll saunter down. How's the bairn anyway?"

"Cracking form. A genius for a father and not a drop of
Scots blood."

"Who's the father then?"

"Bagpipe blower. Listen, if you do look in, remember
what Mayor Daley said. 'The policeman isn't there to
create disorder, the policeman's there to preserve disorder.' "

"Greetings to Sam and Miriam from the land of the
free, you East End disaster, you stewed, slewed eel, you
cowpat in the pasture of the soul."

"Hoots awa', haggis-face."

We hung up, holding the giggles in. Miriam couldn't
say I hadn't tried.

Considering Willie's boast of Glasgow as the cradle of
punch-ups, and the city's tradition of Scots-Irish rivalry,
BAGS night at the Kelvin Hall passed off comparatively
quietly. The press next day was unexcited. The *Telegraph*
carried most, a quarter of a column, and *The Times* only
marginally less, but the others settled for two or three
paragraphs. In most cases the story was not the brawling
between born-again stewards and Glasgow's feminists, gays,
lefties, and vegetarians, or the two arrests, but the concus-
sion of a policeman, felled in the affray by a blow from a
banner.

The press reports are in the file. The *Post* was more
inventive than most. If they're short of a human interest

angle on the *Post* they make one up, though basically they were accurate enough. I don't remember the exact wording. Something as follows.

One of Scotland's toughest policemen will be back at his desk today with his head in bandages after being knocked cold by a Peace and Love banner during fighting at a born-again evangelism rally in Glasgow last night.

Colleagues carried rugged Detective Superintendent Willie "Gangbuster" Smith from the Kelvin Hall after the pole of the banner broke over his head. Fighting erupted between demonstrators and stewards when American preacher the Reverend Jody C. James, 44, star of the Born-Again Gospel Show, called for immediate adoption by NATO of the neutron bomb and the gaoling of homosexuals.

Police arrested two demonstrators. After hospital treatment, Det. Supt. Smith said, "It's part of the job. There are nuts and nuts, and mine takes some cracking."

Willie said nothing of the sort. He never opens his mouth to the press unless he needs them. I phoned him. He wasn't as resentful as he might've been, but I sent him a bottle of Grant's, which made me feel better.

The curious part of the business, though I didn't think too much of it then, was that the by-line on the *Post*'s report was Peter Ramsden. The national dailies don't send a man from London to Glasgow unless he's a specialist on a specialist story, or the story's expected to be headlines. They use their man in Glasgow, or a stringer, or the agencies. Ramsden, a call to the *Post* revealed, wasn't a specialist. He was a workaday general reporter. He'd covered the born-again rally in London, but what was so sensational about them as to justify a reporter following them round full-time?

Something afoot? If there was, I didn't realise it. No one did. Why would we? Ramsden's stories never hinted at Jody James being the chauffeur for the Arabs who went over the cliff, and he never got in touch with us. We'd have needed a crystal ball to have seen a connection. The only tie-in was God, Jody James presumably being religious, and the chauffeur having flogged religious tours. But as I say, we've no God Squad, no experts in the field.

Still, it wasn't many hours, next day in fact, Monday, before we were up to our eyeballs in it, and the Factory's shiny new God Squad—guess who?—was plodding north to soggy Manchester to cast an eye over the goings-on of a Yank preacher, and a homegrown hack from the more sewery reaches of Fleet Street.

FIVE

Two people suspected the Reverend Jody James and the Arabs' chauffeur might be one and the same. My news editor, because I'd told her, and myself. It was Helen who insisted no one else be told. Least of all the police.

I'm not saying Helen's suspicions were profound. I hadn't convinced her because I wasn't wholly convinced myself. Not yet. But she's an old pro for whom the outside chance of an exclusive is worth the time and money. It isn't her money, after all. For an exclusive at this level, Helen would've invested far more than one lone reporter swanning through the provinces in the shadow of the born-again caravan. But to have put more reporters on the job would've attracted attention, brought the competition in, and possibly alerted the Reverend. As it was, the philosophers of Fleet Street must've assumed the *Post* news desk had lost its marbles, assigning a London reporter to these born-again gigs.

They could've turned out to be right, too, in which case Helen would have shrugged it off. If Jody were simply Jody, above reproach, and for all anyone knew the saviour of a world sliding into the abyss, a new messiah out of the backwoods—then too bad. Back to the office and revelations of the exploitation of Father Christmases during the season of goodwill.

How I was going to convince myself he was the chauffeur was a question I puzzled over. Finally, the only answer was going to be to ask him, and watch his eyes. But if he'd killed four Arabs he might well react with more than his eyes. Arranging a limousine ride, for instance, for the questioner.

I hope I'm not a coward, but the head-on approach failed to appeal. Was I being overimaginative? What a distance I'd come from the weddings and prizegivings for the Eastleigh *Examiner!*

Proving that Jody had disposed of the Arabs, finding evidence that'd allow me to write the story, that was another problem, and probably the point at which the police were going to have to be told, so giving every other paper a share in our headlines.

One problem at a time.

When I phoned Helen from Manchester she was neutral Helen, probably with a hangover, and juggling a half-dozen long-shot stories of which mine was but one, and the longest shot of all.

"Peter, dear, are you saved yet?"

"Working on it. I've arrived in the city of light."

"Athens?"

"Our Athens of the north. Apart from a host of born-again, turned-around Americans in hailing distance, nothing thrilling."

"I'd have thought being born once was enough for most of us. As for being turned around, there are laws about that. Are you saying you've not talked to him yet?"

"It's not that easy. He thrives on publicity, and he's good on the paraphernalia of press conferences, and television studios, but not the tap on the shoulder, the notebook at the door of his Mercedes. Maybe there's booze on his breath." This last thought spilled out flippantly, but made me pause. I remembered a whiff of something from the chauffeur on the esplanade. "I tried last night at the Kelvin Hall. He's ringed round by bruisers in red blazers who tell you he's tired, or he's praying."

"Where're they staying?"

"Tudor Inn."

"Where're you?"

"Same. Our man's on the floor above. The Coronet Suite. I've got half the choir and the organist along my corridor."

"Watch the organist, darling. Lock your door or you'll be turned around like a top. Do we get a story tonight?"

"Unlikely. It's individual prayer. Next rally's tomorrow evening."

"*Ne quittez pas,*" Helen said, showing off her telephone French picked up in foreign wars. Someone had arrived in earshot.

When she spoke again it was to sign over and out. News editors never stay more than sixty seconds with any one subject. Perhaps the Thames was on fire.

The Tudor Inn was contemporary posh. Five stars. I wouldn't know where the five stars came from, presumably themselves, they're not mentioned in *Michelin,* or *The Good Food Guide*. Anyway, it wasn't an inn if what's meant by an inn is doxies and Tom Jones, and the only Tudor angle was the Henry VIII bar where the music was piped timbrels and sackbuts, and the sherry was called sack, inaccurately, I think. I knew Manchester, but this was the first time I'd set foot in the Tudor Inn. Here was plushness I didn't know what to do with, all on the *Post*. Until tomorrow's rally I had nothing to do except wallow.

That and discovering whether the Reverend James had murdered four Arabs.

Tomorrow I'd drop in at home and say hello. I could've saved the *Post* a penny or two by putting up at home, but something I'd already learned was that to meet the Reverend I'd do well to stay close, like an assassin.

My Glasgow attempt to get close had been a little feeble, I admit it, but it had been an attempt, beginning with what I gather the Scots call a nip and a chaser in The Calypso, a pub down the road from the Kelvin Hall. Then a second, the first not having done much in making me soldier-brave, and a third, which did, it must've done, because next I was breezing past doorkeepers into the back of the Kelvin Hall, flaunting my union card, which for all the doorkeepers saw of it might've been a Guinness label, and telling them, "Press . . . the *Post* . . . appointment with the Reverend James . . ." This was half an hour before curtain-up on BAGS, Great Awakening, Glasgow, with the queues of Christians stamping their feet in the snow. One of the flunkeys saluted and pointed me the way to the Green Room area and artistes' room number one.

Outside of which, in the corridor, stood this scrubbed, cropped steward in a red blazer, doing nothing. Except what he was doing was being there. He served much the same purpose as Hadrian's Wall.

"*Post*, from London, quick word with the Reverend James."

I'm afraid that subsequent emphasis on our three million readers, and how delighted the Reverend Minister would be to see me, had no effect. A second scarlet blazer had materialised behind me, and a third appeared like a conjuring trick, all lovingly smiling and nodding, standing too close to me, and not listening. Pastor James required this time for preparatory reflection and communing with the Lord, sir, explained the first scarlet blazer, smiling, standing in front of artistes' room number one with his hands clasped in front of his fly. Perhaps later there might be opportunities for the Pastor to autograph any texts I might care to buy, sir. He was oddly chinless, but from where I stood that looked his only weak spot, the rest of him being solid. About two hundred and twenty pounds, I judged, of World Cup goalkeeper material.

The smile of the second was wide enough to reveal a gold molar. The third, carrying a stack of born-again texts costing a pound apiece, said, "Your donation will help change the world, sir." It was these "sirs" more than their scoured, shaved, smiling, bullock bulk which made the air chilly. To my lasting satisfaction I told the book-seller no, thanks all the same.

Whatever else, the First Born-Again Church of God has never to this day had a penny out of me, not even at their Little Rock headquarters, Creation World.

Still, they were telling me no, and they were not to be trifled with, holy as they were. Afterwards, I tried to work out whether holiness could be reconciled with menace and decided, yes, it could, only you didn't call it menace, you called it self-protection, reasonably. Celebrities these days need bodyguards as much as they need air and water if they're going to be safe from fans tearing the hair from their heads, or fanatics shooting them between the eyes. I've never met David Bowie, though of course I easily might, one day, but I understand he has six tax-deductible bodyguards. The Reverend James wasn't in that class, but he was climbing, and he was contentious enough to have attracted hostility as well as applause, and you don't guard yourself against dingbats by hiring ballerinas in tutus, no matter what circuit you're on—showbiz, political, or holy.

A fourth and fifth steward had appeared by the time, a minute after I'd arrived, I was shrugging, pirouetting, and retreating.

The failure left me more apprehensive rather than less. All right, perhaps it was temporary and tactical, but nonetheless it was a failure, and depressing. That's how it is when you have to do something you hate, whether telling a girl it's finished, or making a complaint when you're not sure you're justified, or interviewing someone you know might break down, or turn nasty. The longer you put it off, and the more often you fail, the harder it becomes. Hardest of all is when you've plenty of time, as I had, because then you keep postponing, and the more you postpone the more excuses you invent for doing nothing. My excuse for doing nothing further in Glasgow had been that shortly after the cold shoulder from the stewards I had a story. The rest of the press had it too, the brawling and the copper being knocked out, but my existence was justified for the time being.

But now Manchester. If sooner or later I didn't tackle His Pastorship and see if his eyes clouded over, what was I doing here? Another week and he'd be off back to the States. So at six o'clock I was seated in the lush plushery of the foyer at the Tudor Inn with a pot of tea and *The Evening News*, watching the passing show, and the lifts, and when the Reverend Jody C. James and his bodyguard stepped out I hiked the newspaper up, in front of my face for all the world as if I were some hit man or secret agent out of every second suspense film you ever saw.

From the glimpse I'd had there was a gang of them, perhaps eight or nine, including two women. The big

chinless steward and the one with the gold molar led, with
the Reverend a step behind, flanked by heavyweights, and
the rest in the rear. The Reverend had an upright stride and
s smile like news of tax cuts ahead. His black overcoat
with astrakhan collar and the white silk scarf round his
throat gave him the air of a patron of the opera. The
stewards wore mohair overcoats and suits which no doubt
drew less attention than their scarlet jackets, though if the
purpose had been anonymity they'd have done better to
have split up or, better still, stayed in their rooms. Bunched
as they were, alert and shining, regarded with curiosity by
idlers in the foyer, they might've been a prosperous jazz
band bound for a recording session, or the Hungarian
boxing team with lady guides. I lowered my newspaper an
inch and looked over its edge at exactly the wrong moment.

The eyes of Chinless, striding through the foyer, his
head turned, were on mine. Perhaps they were trained to
be alert to anyone tucked behind a newspaper. Too late to
hoist the newspaper high again, too confused to fold it and
give him a wave. So I continued to peer at him over the
brim. His gaze shifted elsewhere. In another moment all I
could see was their backs filing out of the lobby into the
forecourt.

I gave them a moment, then followed. In the bright
forecourt I watched the Reverend and his immediate co-
horts being driven off in one taxi, the remainder climbing
into two other taxis. I hung back, then approached the
commissionaire who'd been opening and shutting doors.
Shedding my National Theatre vowels, I gave him my
homeliest Manchester.

"They're t' American evangelists and ah'm press—t'
Post. Dost tha know where they're off to?"

He pretended he didn't. He had a wart on his nose like
Oliver Cromwell. I fed a banknote into his palm.

"Likely t' owd church," he said, which from one
Mancunian to another is shorthand for the Collegiate Church
of St. Mary—the cathedral.

For a visiting man of God with an evening to kill, the
cathedral well might be where he'd be off to. I was
puzzled all the same, having by now convinced myself,

almost, that Jody James was a man of the devil, and where he and his staff were off to in their sober gear was more likely to be some fleshpot where varieties of pot would be served along with the wine, women, and song. I set out on foot because in the rush hour feet weren't going to be that much slower than a taxi. I still didn't believe I'd find them in the cathedral.

But there they were. I stood in the half-dark to one side of the west door, watching them perambulate in slow, scattered twos and threes, observing the fan vaulting, the minstrel angel bosses, the choir stalls. The Reverend James stood in company near the communion rail, hands behind his back, regarding the clerestory windows as though in meditation. If it were he. The lighting was dim, and though the cathedral is small as cathedrals go, we were at opposite ends of the nave. Not for the first time I wondered if I might've been mistaken, if Jody-boy might not be the genuine article.

So far he'd been above reproach. Even if I'd missed something, if houris awaited him in his Coronet Suite, nothing was going to happen here in this hallowed sanctuary. He was not behind closed doors or totally surrounded by stewards. Now was as good a time as any for my instant interview.

As I started forward towards the centre aisle a figure from the dark somewhere to my left started in the same direction. We reached the aisle at almost the same moment but with this fellow a couple of steps in front, which allowed him to halt and face me from between the rear pews, barring my way.

Chinless, of course. Mohair overcoat, shoulders like a ship's deck, hands lightly clasped in front of him, relaxed and affable. When I tried to step past he took a diagonal pace back, which kept him squarely facing me.

"Excuse me," I said, sidestepping.

He sidestepped. We might've been rehearsing a minuet. My fists clenched. While I think it fair to say I'm essentially artistic and intellectual, I'm not a weed. Once, indeed, I'd punched a chauffeur and knocked one of his teeth out. Sidestepping again, more nimbly this time, I dipped my shoulder and sidled through the gap between Chinless and the end of the pew. Except that suddenly there was no gap. Sideways on I moved into immovable overcoat and chinlessness.

He didn't say anything. He didn't need to. What stopped me lashing out was not entirely our being on holy ground. Common sense, I've always thought, as well as the pen, is mightier than the sword. On that one occasion when I had hit someone—I have the scar on my forefinger—much good had it done me.

"D'you mind?" I said. "You're not in Little Rock now. I'd like a word with your Mr. James."

"The Pastor is at prayer, sir."

"When he's finished then." He wasn't at prayer, he was looking at windows and inscriptions. "Presumably he finishes."

"A press conference is scheduled for Saturday, sir. We sincerely hope you'll be present."

"Sincerely, thanks."

"You're welcome."

You're welcome. How tiresome the automatic responses of the uneducated! Crab-wise I scuttled along the rear pew. The centre aisle was not the only aisle giving access to the holy Pastor. I was aware of the steward's company in the pew in front, keeping pace. Though not vast, the cathedral has the widest nave of any in the country, so while scuttling I had time to consider alternatives, such as doubling back, or climbing over the pews, or hurdling them.

And then what?

Accompanied, I pressed on, wondering when vergers would converge, and whether they'd be on my side or Chinless's. When I reached the side aisle I was unable to enter it because another mohair overcoat stood there. He might've been the one with the molar, but since he wasn't smiling, he wasn't glinting, so I couldn't be sure.

"I'm the press!" I told him. "All I'm asking is a word with Mr. James!"

"Saturday, sir," Chinless said in my ear. He wasn't even out of breath. "If you let me have your name, I'll make sure you receive an invitation."

Between sandstone pillars a verger, or beadle, someone in a gown—the bishop for all I knew—was hurrying towards us with that tense, ungainly gait of someone trying not to seem to be hurrying, like a restaurant manager when rowdies start throwing bread. Perhaps I should've stayed, put my case to him. But what could he have done?

"All right, Saturday," I mumbled.

The steward blocking my way stepped back, and I left the cathedral without leaving my name. If they wanted it, they could sodding find it out for themselves.

Bloody, figuratively speaking, but unbowed. Bloody-minded certainly, simmeringly bloody-minded, my first victim being the head waiter who welcomed and led me, bathed and lotioned, to a table not unadjacent to a grand piano.

"No thanks." I pointed to a more central table. "That one."

He hesitated, about to inform me that the more central table was reserved for the Norwegian ambassador, or that it wobbled. Then he led through airy spaces to the table and slid out a chair, which I ignored. I sat at the opposite end of the table from where I could watch, a table or two distant, the born-again gospel singers.

The two at the nearest table were the token black and the bony, frizzed redhead. They couldn't have been there many minutes because they were engrossed in menus, and no comestibles were yet in sight, though now a waiter was bearing down with a jug of water, which was presumably what they drank. The man wore a dark suit and tie, and the girl something sedate and boring, I don't remember what. She didn't bore me though. For instance, her hair looked untidy rather than frizzed, as if she'd lost patience and couldn't be bothered. I liked that. She wasn't too engrossed in the menu either, but flicking the pages. She had the restless air of one who might sooner have been doing a parachute jump, or at least been out on the town, than sitting in this respectful dining room.

Beyond them, sharing crowded tables, demure, unrestless singers in sombre suits and dresses were eating what looked

to be steaks and salad, with milk. Other customers held
my attention not at all: Norwegian ambassadors and their
wives, cotton tycoons suffering from imports from Hong
Kong. The black and the frizzed redhead had not been
ostracized, I imagined, from the main body of the choir.
Simply, there was no room at the larger tables.

But if anyone were to be ostracized, they were perhaps
the obvious choice. He black, she with her bones and
bull-by-the-horns air, as if she alone might've been prepared, unrehearsed, to take on a tricky descant, and if she
hit some wrong notes, why then, she'd try again. Game, I
thought, might be the word, for no better reason than a
wordsmith's frivolous wordplay I ordered the game soup.
Also lamb cutlets and a half bottle of claret, I think it may
have been the Margaux. Straightaway I decided that after
what I'd been through in the cathedral, and considering all
the aggravation, not to say menace, of this reporting job,
now was no time for half measures, so I told the somme-
lier to make it the full bottle. I pride myself on knowing a
fair amount about the grape, and naturally I'm able to hold
my liquor. On mornings after, I can name every wine of
the evening before, assuming they were worth remembering, and recall them on my palate, though I will have
forgotten such trivia as whether the girl wore jeans or a
kimono.

Certain experiences, encounters, and people, I also remember acutely, almost photographically. So when the
Reverend appeared in the dining room, even though I
could've told you nothing about his eyes except they were
two, I was surer than ever he was my chauffeur.

This was after the soup, awaiting the lamb, and avoiding looking at young Frizzy. She'd grown aware of my
awareness. She'd mentioned me to her companion, she
must have, because he too was aware, casting towards me
glances so blank there was no telling what was in his mind,
whether he was wondering if he might have to defend her
honour, or if there might be a chance of selling it. Though
I fancied her, I'd no intention of pressing my pagan affec-
tions on her. The stewards were chore enough without my
joining battle with the choir.

So instead of realising that chatting up a chorister just might lead to an introduction to Jody himself, a thought which was another three or four minutes in dawning, I was concentrating on the wine, and a textiles baron who was having problems with a dish of elastic pasta. Meanwhile there was a flurry of activity as staff greeted and guided the Reverend and his retinue through the dining room towards a long, reserved table. Smiling, looking about him—I'd not have been amazed if he'd raised two arms and called out, "Praise the Lord!"—he peeled away from the head waiter and threaded between tables in my direction, attended by cool bruisers.

My direction, but not to me. He had noticed his choir, at whose tables he halted, beaming, to place hands on shoulders and to mouth benisons, or advice that the cathedral was a must, or reminders that fornication was a no-no, and rehearsal for sopranos would be at ten sharp tomorrow, noon for baritones. Royalty finding a word for as many as possible. Mess officer of the day doing the rounds.

He raised a hand to the black and the redhead two tables away. They raised their hands in return. They were pig-in-the-middle between the Reverend and myself, and it seemed to me his gaze wavered, looking beyond them. He stood with hand uplifted in salute, regarding me, and his smile slipping, or so I thought. But immediately the smile was once more radiant and he'd turned away, striding on, and whether he'd remembered me from somewhere, such as a wet esplanade, I couldn't have said.

No question that his chinless flanker knew me. He stared impassively, then moved on with his chief.

After the cutlets, and some cheese, I stood up. The bottle was empty, or very nearly. The black and Frizzy would've supposed I was on my way out, but I was on my way over. They were eating ice cream.

"Excuse me, I'm the press, the *Post,* covering your campaign, enjoying it enormously, most impressive, immensely successful, sure you'll agree, quick word, mind if I sit down?"

I was already sitting down. Relaxed, not ingratiating, the correct balance of formality and friendliness, peppering them, the raw colonials, with crisp consonants and round vowels. To be honest, the wine had been unusually robust, at least thirteen degrees. If I'd not sat down I'd have fallen down.

"Help yourself," the man said.

"Peter Ramsden . . ."

"Babby Faster," he said in a ripe bass, stretching out his hand. He might've meant Bobby Foster, though there was no knowing. "Pet Aversion."

"Sorry?"

"Hi," said the girl.

"Good evening."

Hands were shaken across the table. Pet Aversion's handshake was not vice-like, but neither was it the offer of the washing-up cloth. Her response to my presence I'd have described as interested but not yet overwhelmed. In spite of what Babby believed, her name surely wasn't Pet Aversion. Petty Virgin, possibly? Virgin on the bizarre, I was tempted to throw out, though I doubt they'd have got it. I chose to concentrate, pretend to, on the bloke, if I could understand anything he said. Let the magic work indirectly. Her boniness failed to put me off. The bright, grass-green eyes went very nicely thank you with her red hair. Reddish anyway, red-brown, coppery.

Born-again she might be, the Lord her exclusive love, but she had Peter Ramsden as her votary, and if she needed a convert, I was her man. She'd picked up her spoon and was pressing on with her ice cream.

"Heard you, saw you, at the Princess Hall, and Glasgow, be covering you again tomorrow, looking forward, slot of interest, yes, on the *Posht*," I told the bloke. "*Post*."

"I'd not have said the room was going round, but it was tilting, and there were two Babby Fasters where one would've done perfectly well. He interested me not at all. He was a groomed, polite hunk of a man, in perfect control of himself, which I'm afraid I wasn't. If I were to say he appeared interested in me, that his gravy eyes never left me, that might be being wise after the event, because

I'd not swear I was aware of it at the time. I was aware only of Frizzy.

"Like to do," I told him, "an in-depth interview with the Relevant James." The nearest the *Post* got to in-depth anything was starlets' cleavage across six columns. "One of the great men of our time. An earth-shifter. That's to say, world-shifter. Mover. I'm going to nail the lie he's a crazy racist. Fingers in your till up to his armpits. I'll nail that one. And Pithley. Four dead caliphs. Goin' to nail—"

"Pardon me," interrupted a civil voice, not Babby's, but somewhere above, to my right.

I didn't need to look because I'd guessed who. I looked anyway, Chinless. He wasn't looking at me. He was smiling at Babby and Pet Aversion.

"The Pastor," he said, "would consider it a privilege if you'd both consent to join him at his table."

"I accept," I said.

He ignored me, so I ignored him. I pushed back my chair and set off in the direction of His Pastorship's table at a pace as brisk as was compatible with staying roughly upright. I weaved between tables, a hand on the back of occasional vacant chairs to steady myself, and once on the bare upper arm of the wife of a cotton king, just above the vaccination mark.

"So sorry."

I sensed Chinless on my heels but didn't look round. At Jody James's table a steward seated at the near end had recognised me and was rising. I changed course for the far end, watching the Reverend, who was watching me. He sat in the centre seat, naturally, like Jesus at the Last Supper. Other stewards were pushing their chairs back, too late, because I'd rounded the end of the table, and anyway they'd have been even less eager for a roughhouse here, I judged, than in the cathedral.

"Excuse me, Reverend James? I'm the press, the *Post*, been hoping for a word with you, would that be all right?"

His eyes were the palest blue, like the sky over the sea at Eastleigh on a good day. Mesmeric too, passionately skewering me, unless it was the effect of the wine. My wine. He had water. If he'd had whiskies as aperitifs he'd

drowned the pong with cologne. He wasn't wearing a
cheese-cutter cap, tunic, and three-day beard either, and if
he opened his mouth he wasn't going to be gap-toothed.
But he was my man. I was convinced he knew me too, and
if he wasn't rolling his blue eyes in terror of a material
witness from his killer days, that was because he'd had
ample warning and time to compose himself.

No doubt he considered me no threat anyway. He
might've recognised me at the press table at his rallies in
London and Glasgow. He'd have been kept informed of
my attempts to speak to him at the Kelvin Hall, and in the
cathedral.

I stood stooping between him and one of the female
guides in the chair to his right, with Chinless behind me.
Jody was looking up at me with his blue, hypnotist's eyes.

"My editor's very enthusiastic," I said. "Your campaign, our circulation—"

"The Lord in his wisdom allots a time and place for
everything," the Reverend sonorously informed me. "Now
we are at supper."

"Bon appetit," I said. Everything was tilting. It was
like being at sea. "After you've supped then? Ten o'clock
in the lobby?"

"Ten o'clock in the lobby—tomorrow morning, Mr.
Ramsden. An immeasurable privilege."

"All right."

Had I been more clear-headed I might've been less
quick in supposing it'd be all right. Neither did it register
that he knew my name and willingly had let me know he
knew. All I was aware of in those moments was the tilting
deck, and how privileged these born-again people were
always feeling. Privileged that the black and the girl should
consent to join them at his table. Immeasurably privileged
that I should want an interview.

I turned, sneered at Chinless, and smiled at Babby and
Pet Aversion, whose company at the Reverend's table,
where they'd be secure against reporters, probably wouldn't
be required now that Ramsden of the *Post,* formerly of
Eastleigh, its *Examiner* and its esplanade, was on his way
out, tacking for the exit.

* * *

Philo L. Abbott, 27. Born, Pocahontas, Ark. Educ., Ouachita Baptist University, Arkadelphia, Ark.

Clyde Gasp, 22. Born, Clarksville, Ark. Educ. Manhattan School of Music, Riverside, N.Y.

Alphabetically and chauvinistically listed, basses, baritones, and tenors preceding contraltos and sopranos, the names of the born-again choir in a handout I'd retrieved from the press kit were as exotic, very nearly, as those of the staff listed at the front of *Time*, with the exception of workaday, English-sounding Bobby Foster. So were some of their alma maters. College of the Ozarks. Calvary Bible. Oral Roberts University. I lay on my bed with the handout feeling very unwell. The print was fuzzy, and so far I'd only skimmed, but among the contraltos and sopranos I'd found neither an Aversion nor a Virgin.

I'd turned on the telly because it was there, the sound silent because of my head. Babby, a bass, he was there too. In the handout, not on the telly. Presumably this was Babby. Robert Foster, 29. Born, Chattanooga, Tenn. Educ., University of California, Berkeley, Calif.

Tennessee made sense. Was Tennessee adjacent to Arkansas? Somewhere in Tennessee in the twenties was where there'd been that monkey trial. What was his name? A biology schoolteacher who'd brought down the wrath of the fundamentalists and the law because he'd taught Darwinism.

Darwinianism?

Scopes. The Scopes trial.

Plus ça change.

More with my ears than my eyes I went again through the women's names. Jean Quincey Levinski . . . Jo-Jane Rumbelow . . .

On the screen a character in a cravat was trailing round an art gallery, mutely mouthing. The camera homed in on a cupid's foot, a bag of shot grouse.

Roberta Kneeschorn . . . Chesyl Martha Lung . . . Petal Merchant . . .

Ha.

Last but one of the sopranos. Penultimate Petal. Coal

merchants I'd heard of, petal merchants never. Ho-ho. I
declaimed the name aloud, several times. I needed aspirin,
Fernet Branca, and a week's sleep.

Peter Ramsden, sick hack, idiot.

She was twenty-four, born in Hope, Arkansas—Arkansas
seemed to be the catchment area for most of the choir,
reasonably enough—and educated at Southern Baptist
Junior College, Walnut Ridge, Arkansas. I reached for the
telephone, apologised to the switchboard girl for having
mislaid the room number of Miss Merchant, but seemed to
recall, I said, taking great care of my consonants, it might
be in the one-twenty one-thirty range. If she'd be so kind.

"One moment, dear, see what we can do." After the
moment, "Here we are, dear. One-two-eight. Like me to
try it for you?"

"Please." On the screen the character in the cravat was
going berserk over the profile of a Genoese marquesa.

"Yes," a girl breathed in my ear. Not the switchboard
girl.

"Hello? Petal Merchant?"

"Who's that?"

"The *Post*. Petal? We met at supper." Pause for diges-
tion. "I'm doing this feature on your church. Tried to tell
you. The Reverend's enthusiastic, I've an interview with
him tomorrow. But the singer's angle, he's especially for
that, he'd like me to pick a singer. For an interview. Might
we have a cup of cocoa or something and a chat? If it's not
too late?"

A further pause. I waited. The cravat character was
practically banging his head against the marquesa in ecstasy.

The girl in my ear said, "I think you have the wrong
number."

I thought I hadn't. "The Reverend James's keen as
mustard. I'm room one twenty-one. One-two-one. Or I
could come to you. Are you sharing? If you'd rather, we
could meet downstairs, the lobby, bring a friend—hello?"

She had hung up.

A merciful escape for us both, I worked at convincing
myself. Nothing much in the way of spiritual awakening
awaited Petal Merchant from a heathen reporter on a tit-and-

bum rag, and though I'd not have said no to a night of
romance, I wasn't feeling in top form, definitely the wine'd
had bottle fatigue, or there may have been insufficient
ullage, and the chance of dalliance with any of the BAGS
ladies, even with this most fidgety of the entourage, had
never been better than remote.

Pity all the same. If hand-holding would've had to have
been prefaced by a hymn, so be it. I'd have sung like a
lark.

And it came to pass that after perfunctory ablutions and
the donning of the pointlessly sexy silk pyjamas from the
Burlington Arcade, there sounded the lightest of taps on
my locked door, causing me to reflect as follows: Good
heavens, good girl, she's even fidgetier than she looks,
I've picked the winner, the one questionable, possible
bruised, even slightly maggoty, but unquestionably delicious windfall in the otherwise machine-garnered, computer-
graded, born-again barrel.

She was so eager that the door was pushed open in the
instant I unlocked it.

Chinless and a brace of his lieutenants surged in, the last
one in closing the door behind him.

Chinless said, "Making a nuisance of yourself to Pastor
James is one thing, sir. Insulting our womenfolk is another. This warning is for your own good, I'm sure you'll
agree."

He punched me in the belly, brought his knee up into
my face, then kicked my head, which anyone would agree,
Chinless included, falls in the category of gratuitous violence.

SIX

Chief inspectors move in a mysterious way, their wonders to perform (*recorded P.O. Kremer in shorthand, pausing to interrupt the policeman's long hand in its wandering, return her skirt over her knee, and say, "Cut it out, sir"*).

No mystery in my boarding the afternoon train to Manchester, though I'm not denying there were one or two raised eyebrows. Tuesday afternoon it was, in time to catch the born-again rally that evening, if I felt up to it.

There'd been what sounded like a plea for help on behalf of the reporter, Ramsden. Since he wasn't my department I made a couple of overdue immigration visits, my excuse for getting out of London. The real reason for the excursion north wasn't immigration, or Ramsden, but the prospect of a night's sleep away from Sam, Sam, horrible old man. Miriam does the feeding but I do the collecting and putting back. Not the foggiest how this routine started but it was an error because I'm stuck with it. What the Peckover household requires is an assertion of male supremacy.

I'm not too clear how word about the reporter reached us. The start was a phone call to the *Post*. The call was anonymous, and the *Post* wasn't the *Post*, the national daily, but the Burnley *Post*, near Manchester. But the caller wanted Ramsden's *Post* so whoever she was she can't have known much about him, not knowing which *Post* he worked for. Probably called the first *Post* she found in the directory.

She, right. The bloke on the Burnley *Post* who took the

call said she was a she and American, or sounded American, and what she said was, "Please take Peter Ramsden off the born-again campaign assignment or they'll break his legs." According to the Burnley *Post* bloke, newspapers here don't have assignments, they've never heard the word. Americans might have assignments but what we have are stories or jobs.

That's all she said, then rang off. We know now who she was but we didn't then. Since she'd mentioned the born-again tour, and was American, the guess was she might've been one of them, which narrowed the field to a couple of score of singers, stewardesses, programme sellers, and secretaries, all staying at the Tudor Inn. The Burnley *Post* had never heard of Peter Ramsden and passed the message to the Burnley police, who dug up a Peter Ramsden on the *Post* in London. They passed this snippet to the Yard because they're lazy buggers and wanted nothing more to do with it.

Fair enough. Ramsden was a London staff man. Still, all they'd have had to do was ring the *Post* to find out what was going on, which is what our CID did. Far as the *Post* knew, nothing was going on. Ramsden was alive and well and in Manchester covering the evangelicals. They'd check with him and call back if there were any problems.

No problems. They didn't call back, and the CID didn't call them back.

The American woman's call had been pretty meaningless. Who were "they" who were going to break the reporter's legs? His legs hadn't been broken, not as far as anyone knew. No crime, no complaint. We get hundreds of alarms like this. I wish I'd a quid for every time someone'd wanted to break a reporter's legs. But at the end of the day reporters' legs have a way of staying intact. So that should've been the end of it.

Enter Buggins, who at this point hadn't heard of any of this. First, rather, enter Detective Sergeant Terry Sutton, flogging raffle tickets.

"Support your Metropolitan Police rugby dance, sir. Unrepeatable prizes. Frozen turkey, frozen port-type wine, two frozen gallery seats for the *Messiah*—"

"Haven't you got any work to do?" I was at my desk, minding my business, sweating over a poem about love and ageing which was a disaster but which I hadn't yet been able to bring myself to abandon.

> There's still a purity about you,
> Colonel's daughter, did no one rout you?

"You don't have to dance, sir. You don't even have to go. All you have to do is buy three books of tickets."

I slid the poem under the blotter and told him, "Forgery's three floors down, mate. Illegal immigrants only here, and we're up to our eyes."

"Pouring in, are they?" He was very cheerful. Christmas was a month away but Sutton's young enough to go weak at thoughts of Santa Claus. His big rugby player's face brightened further. "Did you hear your reporter chum Ramsden's going to get his legs broken by the singing missionaries?"

"He's not my chum, chum. Never even met him. What're you talking about?"

"The born-again lot up in Manchester. There was a tip-off about the wrath to come and broken bones for Ramsden if he doesn't leave off writing about them. Could've come from the evangelists themselves. One of our thinkers in Intelligence rang the *Post* but they knew nothing."

"When?"

"Half an hour ago. Incidentally, most generous and giving they are in the information room. As for Records, they practically bought me out. You're lucky, still a few left, sir. Two quid a book."

"Bloody hell."

"Three for a fiver?"

"Go away."

"One ticket, tenpence?"

"Forgeries, are they?"

I shelled out two quid and after he'd left retrieved the paper from under the blotter.

> A steely chastity runs through you,
> Mechanic's child, who now will screw you?

October ripeness mists the real you,
Greengrocer girl, who's left to feel you?

Peel you? Make a meal of you? Into the wastepaper basket it went. Out came the London directory. Letter P.

I got first an Australian with his mouth full of pastry who addressed me as Matey and kept telling me I had the wrong number. After a quiet word with him about obstruction, false evidence, and bestiality, I got this old girl with a voice like the sound of a soda syphon running dry. She was the news editor, name of Helen Goodenough, who'd already told all she knew to some constable, she said, apart from Peter Ramsden having just phoned in saying he'd be sending a story on the evening rally, if there was a story. Codswallop, her opinion, the so-called call about breaking legs. Some ditched girl friend of Peter's, fantasizing. But any further help she could give, only too pleased. Thank you, good-bye.

"Hold on." I'd not like to have tried snatching this one's handbag. "When Ramsden phoned in just now he knew about the call, did he?"

"No."

"But you told him."

"I-mentioned it."

"What was his reaction?"

"Nothing. Amused."

"He found it funny?"

"Not incapacitating. But men of God threatening to savage him, it has its ludicrous side. Or would if it were true."

"Supposing it were true. What reason would they have?"

"They wouldn't."

"You know Ramsden. I don't. What's he been up to?"

"Doing his job. Perhaps they don't like his coverage. Heavy on the demonstrating, light on God."

"Haven't all the papers been heavy on the demonstrating?"

"Perhaps they've all been threatened with broken legs."

"So you're keeping him on the story."

"I don't see any reason why we shouldn't."

"Slim pickings, isn't it, for the effort you're making?

Tying up a reporter for a week on four rallies? What're you hoping for?''

"A policeman was knocked out in Glasgow. That was a nice story."

"Where is he now?"

"Who?"

"Ramsden."

"The Tudor Inn."

That could be true. The rest took some swallowing. Even God-bothering fanatics don't consider breaking a journalist's legs because of the emphasis of his stories. If they did, the journalist in question would have to be peculiar to think it amusing.

As for having a reporter on the campaign full-time, she hadn't answered that. What at the Factory we're pleased to call withholding of information. Madam and Ramsden presumably thought they were onto something. The authentic dirt on the First Born-Again Church of God.

Nothing new, the press forking up the dirt until they've enough for headlines. Hoarding it when they should be passing it to us.

If that sounds like sour grapes, it isn't, it's all one to me. A bulwark of democracy, the media, I know that, and I believe it. But the police are a bulwark of democracy too. I've seen toe-rags who ought to have been put in solitary getting away with it because some reporter on the make cocked it up for us, and the same crummy crook fetching up with a five-figure cheque for his story. All right, they're a mixed bunch, the press and telly, some are the salt of the earth, but most of my best friends don't happen to be reporters. They don't happen to be coppers either, but we're less hypocritical, my opinion anyway. You meet journalists who're strong on civic duty and moral responsibility and obligations to society, but they'll cash in on whatever's going when it suits them, and they're the first to whine and preach about the public's right to know the moment some naïve berk stands up in Parliament to complain about intrusion, or lies, or carrying on vendettas, or trial by newspaper, or paying fat sums to tearaways. Chances were the *Post* had sniffed out some financial fiddle. That was my guess. The Reverend Thing—I couldn't even remember his name—cooking the books. Probably there weren't any books. Anyway, nothing new about the occasional fiddle among men of the cloth. A fiver a throw for leaflets, pass round the collection plate, and into the pocket of Holy Joe.

Holy Jody.

Whoever's business it was, it wasn't Illegal Immigration's. Nothing to do with my files on the families rowing home to Newhaven from sunny Pakistan. If cooking the books was what the *Post* thought it was onto, it wasn't even interesting. And making it my business, even if I were given the green light, wasn't going to change the world.

So I called first my chief super to stress the urgency of liaison visits to Immigration mates in Manchester and Bradford, and I dropped a mention of the born-again rally. The rally might be worth a look, I told him, because I'd be in the area, and as they'd be back in London at the weekend, provoking riots, could be I'd be able to pass a tip or two to Division. I had to mention the rally because for all I knew a news clip might turn up on TV, fifteen seconds of Henry Peckover in the thick of the faithful with his head thrown back and mouth open, singing to the Lord, and I didn't want the chief super unprepared. He wasn't gripped. He said all right, though. He's suffering every kind of middle-age crisis. Weight, wife, whisky, and hardening of the overdraft. He's got an astronomic mortgage, and galactic school fees, shelling out for fencing lessons, bob sleighing, dressage, because he wants his children to marry into royalty.

I called Miriam in her hell's kitchen at the Royal Archaeological Society to explain I was being sent to Manchester on pressing Immigration business. Probably be back tomorrow. I didn't refer to the born-again lot because no wonders were going to be performed. I didn't want her disappointed when I failed to have them deported.

I called this Tudor Inn place to reserve a room. Then Euston for train times.

There were half a dozen reasons why I went north, none

convincing. A night's sleep. Boredom with London in November. Boredom with Immigration. Showing Miriam I was as eager as she that the evangelists be scuppered so Sam could grow up in a world invented by reasonable men, not hillbillies. Irritation with Madam Goodenough, who'd been so determined I should believe she'd got nothing which concerned the police. Passing curiosity about Ramsden. What kind of newshound was it who got told to lay off, or have his legs broken?

Doesn't matter what reason. Point is, chief inspector is just lofty enough to make it possible to move in a mysterious way, so long as you don't make a habit of it.

So there he went, Buggins, Our 'Enry, self-appointed, one-man God Squad with his overnight bag.

Manchester was several degrees colder than London, the people warmer. The hotel staff, for instance. The men at reception at the Tudor Inn were amiable and efficient, the girls were amiable, efficient, and nice to look at, their accents evoking coal fires and high tea of kippers with bread and butter. They didn't actually say to me, "Eeh, bah gum," because it was after all the Tudor Inn, and I was a customer, but they'd have been saying it to each other all the time. Odd, really, because I did my share of soccer crowd control in my uniform days, and the window-smashing, tyre-slashing, urinating yobbos who came down with Manchester United were the worst of the lot.

A toothsome, plumpish miss full of Lancashire hotpot looked after me across the counter, seeking in a register, then in lists from a file, the room number of Peter Ramsden.

"Here, one twenty-two, but he's gone," she said. "He paid his bill and left this morning."

"Did he mention where he was going?"

"Couldn't say. Was he the journalist? The one had the accident?"

"That's him." Accident? "Any of you know anything about it? I'd been hoping for a word with him."

"Nancy might. Can you wait a second?"

All the time in the world, love. I watched her retreat to

an alcove where a girl in a mustardy jersey sat at a desk tapping a calculator. Assuming Ramsden's accident was before he'd paid and gone, had he gone on his own two legs, or been wheeled out?

"It was his face, quite nasty." Nancy was as pretty as the first girl, though her fringe could've done with a trim. I doubted she could see me. "I mean, not ugly or anything, but his eye and lip."

"Legs all right?"

"Legs? What was wrong with his legs?"

Under her mustard jersey she was as plump as the first girl. What did they eat in Manchester—Yorkshire pudding? The best Yorkshire pudding's made in Lancashire, according to Lancashire people. I read once about an all-comers world Yorkshire pudding competition in Leeds which was won by a Chinaman. He'd put ginseng in it, or gunpowder, or something.

"He didn't by any chance say how it happened?"

"He slipped getting into the bath, or out of it. He didn't remember. He'd had too much wine."

"He was quite chatty then?"

"I think he thought if he didn't explain I'd imagine he'd been fighting. He was very nice, jokey, considering." She hesitated, colouring, wondering whether she dare tell all. "He said it wouldn't have happened if I'd been there to look after him. In the bath." The colour deepened. She may have lowered her eyes but it was impossible to see. She sounded delighted. "I mean, well, quite jokey, considering."

"Considering his eye and lip?"

"Yes, and he'd been waiting hours to see the Reverend James."

"Right. What happened there exactly?"

"I don't know. A mix-up. Mr. Ramsden was going to meet the American preacher, but he'd left early to visit all these churches and places. They were gone all day. There was a muddle over times."

"Is he back yet, the Reverend James?"

"Oh yes. And left. All of them. There's this religious meeting, the Great Awakening, you know?"

I knew. In less than half an hour, and I hadn't eaten. No time now if I were to catch the evangelists live in performance. Perhaps in the interval. Loaves, fish, and popcorn.

> "Born again!
> Born again!"

For the most part the anthem booming through the loudspeakers emanated from the organ and the arc of red-robed singers on the distant stage, where there'd have been microphones. But a congregation two to three thousand strong was on its feet helping the singing along. I took off my hat and sidled down a side aisle in the direction of the stage, which ought to be where I'd find the press. I wasn't the only one who'd arrived late. I was in the thick of Christians with sleet in their hair looking for a spare seat, and scrubbed young men and women in scarlet jackets trying to guide us.

> "Fight for the right
> To be men—
> Born again!"

Not that it mattered, but I'd still have missed curtain-up even if I hadn't spent ten minutes phoning the *Post*. I'd simply wanted to ask Madam Goodenough if her Peter Ramsden expected to be there. As she probably knew, I was going to tell her he'd signed out of the Tudor Inn, and though she might be indifferent to threats of broken legs, I'd no objection to showing myself at the rally, making my presence known to such lurking leg-breakers as might exist.

Helen Goodenough had evidently signed out too, out of the newsroom and into the White Swan where I might reach her, said some assistant night editor. Far as he was aware, yes, Peter was covering the rally, and of course he'd checked out of his hotel, he'd be coming back to London after he'd phoned his story. Who'd spend the night in Manchester if he could get back to London? Who was it speaking anyway?

I hung up on that. I wasn't unduly concerned about Ramsden's legs, but if the *Post* did happen to be onto something which the Yard should have known about, and we started ringing them up every five minutes, they'd shut the shutters so fast that not a glimmer would get through to us, ever. My real worry had been where I'd find something to eat. At this rally there wasn't so much as a packet of nuts. Only people.

"I can see one there, sir," a bronzed redcoat told me, pointing to a chair in a row of singing Christians.

"Press," I said.

"Straight ahead, sir. Below the platform."

Against the stage, the press table must've been the last remaining accommodation. I counted seven reporters, four of them male, any one of whom could've been Ramsden. No television, but sundry press cameramen, or camerapersons. Not camerawomen anyway, a breed which doesn't exist, and just as well. Newspaper photographers, in my experience, are always men, and debilitated. Probably from lugging about all that equipment. Why don't they use those dinky cameras the size of chocolate bars like tourists and everybody else?

Chocolate bars. Stomach growling, I stayed against the wall. So much silver, gold, and scarlet dangled above the stage that there was severe risk of eyestrain. The singing had ceased, the congregation had sat, and a big, shiny bloke of around my age, wearing a navy-blue suit and red tie, and holding a Bible, stood spotlit in the centre of the stage telling us Nicodemus said we should be born again.

"And the Lord said," he said, " 'How long halt ye between two opinions?' My very dear friends, shall we stand and give thanks?"

Everyone stood while the man talked to the Lord. The Reverend James? The press didn't stand, and the photographers stalked at random, occasionally flashing a bulb. If everyone else had his eyes shut, now might be the moment for whisperingly asking among the press for Ramsden. I could see only the backs of their heads, and now and then a profile, none of which looked damaged from a fall in the bath.

"Right there's the press, sir," a voice murmured. My smiling redcoat was indicating the table.

Either they were highly trained in solicitude towards the press or they wanted us where they could see us.

I slid into a seat at the end of the press table. Apart from sneezing and shuffling, high electric organ notes accompanied the Reverend James's oration. Reporters' eyes turned to me, failed to identify a colleague, and looked away. None was taking notes.

". . . prophet said, 'There ariseth a little cloud out of the sea, like a hand.' But unless we be born again, my friends, that puny old cloud is going to fatten like the watermelons in my yard back home . . ."

Quoth the Preacher. Something of that nature. Nothing Miriam and Sam could've taken exception to.

After more of the same, and prayers for peace, love, and our very lovely Queen Elizabeth of England—his sucking up to the natives was going down well—he retired from stage centre. The arc of gospel singers broke into song.

> "Like the pilot of a plane
> The fireman of a train
> In sunshine or in rain
> We're on our way—
> Born again!"

I leaned along the table and touched the arm of the nearest reporter. "Ramsden, Peter Ramsden, the *Post*—is he here?"

The reporter shook his baffled head and shrugged. Consultation among the other reporters confirmed an ignorance of Peter Ramsden.

He wouldn't be here either, not at the press table, if his face were as Nancy had put it, nasty. He might prefer anonymity in the body of the hall. If there were Manchester United supporters half the audience would have black eyes and split lips. I twisted about and surveyed the hall.

The stewards had posted themselves against the walls at intervals. They were densest on the right, halfway along the aisle down which I'd come. They knew what they were doing because when the demonstration started, that was where. I don't know if they'd identified faces, or noticed folded banners and packets of godless leaflets, but they knew, they were ready, and, give them their due, they moved in like paratroopers.

The demo interrupted the Reverend, Bible aloft, who was lecturing again after songs, prayers, and a Give for God intermission when buckets were passed round for donations. I'd not been attending, I'd been testing pens and pads from one of the briefcases left on the table for us gents and ladies of the press. Far as I was concerned, the rally was less than a sublime experience, but harmless. The Reverend was no more right-wing than one or two politicians I could name, and he didn't foam at the mouth. Live and let live, say I. Not that I'd have cared to pass an evening with him in the pub.

". . . in the days when the land flowed with milk and honey, Lord, before the plague of do-gooders, of milk-and-water liberals and socialists, those who would slay unborn life, all fornicators and abominationists, the money boys who control this great city of yours, gamblers and loafers stealing the last buck from your pocket . . ."

He wasn't entirely coherent, but I'd not have said he was batty. The press seemed to be paying moderate attention, though they still weren't writing anything down. Perhaps this was the sort of stuff which reverberates well on the eardrums but in print isn't so telling. I had the impression he was gathering steam. His "r's" were getting blurred. "Jesus Chwist," and "Sodom and Gomowwah." As low-key demagoguery, I could believe it was the sort of rubbish which could turn the heads of people who wanted their heads turned.

". . . that we of the great strike force of biblical inerrancy who are born again in Jesus stand and be counted, my friends, in this crusade against the pinko traitors and homosexuals—"

"Yeah!" someone in the audience shouted, though whether in revulsion or envy I couldn't have said.

"—and trashy, so-called democrats who would coddle the Russian juggernaut, the Russian communist abortionists—"

"Jackboot slug! Back to your slime!"

A thud and a squeal interrupted this interruption. It came from somewhere halfway back in the auditorium, near the right-hand aisle.

I stood up and looked round. The demonstrators were on their feet, twenty perhaps, grouped and hostile, shouting their unintelligible complaints, and unfurling sheets with slogans, or trying to. Spoiling for a fight. I've seen a million of them. Chairs were toppling. Families who'd arrived to praise the Lord were squeaking and being pushed to the floor. The stewards surged in like a red wave.

If for no other reason than the balance of opposing forces, you can tell when a demo will be relatively calm, and when it's going to be war to the knife. This looked like one in the latter category, and I was having no part of it. A copper in uniform might've caused second thoughts among some in the struggling scrum, but I hadn't a hope. I stuck my hat on my head, managed one step in the direction of the farther aisle, away from the brawling, and walked head on into a steward.

"If you'll keep your seat, sir," he suggested, arms lifted like a red penguin, crowding me back to my chair. He was so confident I'd not try to bypass him that he wasn't even looking at me, he was watching the fighting, probably trying to decide whether he should run and pitch in or stay put in defence of the Reverend James onstage.

He was right anyway, I didn't try to bypass him. I was tempted to slap his cheek with my press kit, but I didn't do that either. On earth, peace, goodwill towards men. The Reverend should've tried that as his text one day. I stepped back and strode for the near aisle. If the penguin's flipper was now going to land on my shoulder, time enough to worry when it happened.

It didn't. Ahead, scrummaging blocked the aisle. Terry Sutton would've loved it. Personally, I'd sooner an evening by the fire, Sam sleeping, the lady wife knitting something intricate. But the scrapping didn't deter me. If you keep your eyes open, and blunt instruments and lapel badges out of sight, you can get through or round such brawls, even one as emotional as this.

Which I did. Which wasn't to say I didn't know whose side I was on, which was the side of Miriam and all who believe the world's round. I'd not have objected to putting a furtive boot in. There was punching, kicking, tearing of shirts and skirts, and as many of the opposing armies on the floor as upright. Beyond the mêlée an emergency exit door had been opened into the night, and through it stewards were flinging demonstrators. No sooner had they been flung than back they came, heads down, arms windmilling.

Courage and passion aren't enough though. The disadvantage demonstrators of this lefty, anti-BAGS ilk are at, when it comes to mixing it, is that half are women, and most of the rest are seven-stone weaklings. Spidery, anoretic creatures, undernourished and underage, with spectacles and skinny, Trotsky tufts of beard. I noticed one who wasn't. There's always one stevedore. But the redcoats had spotted him too. Three of them had him pinned against the wall.

Another disadvantage for these Manchester lefties was they'd taken on a team trained in unarmed combat.

Even as I edged, ducked, avoiding lurching bodies, hopped over limbs, something hacked my shin, someone cannoned into my back, and I had to chop away at a hand which grabbed my sleeve. The press kit I found I was carrying I crumpled into a pocket so that both hands might be free, just in case. From the stage the singers had launched into a new song. Bully for them, though I wasn't about to rush back and congratulate them on their sang-froid. I'd negotiated the worst of the war. Only isolated skirmishes remained between me and the doors. A redcoat was frog-marching a bloodied youth into the sleet. Another redcoat was slapping a girl's face. Forehand, backhand . . . forehand, backhand . . .

I don't know, maybe she deserved it. Maybe she'd bitten his ear off, though far as I could see he didn't look damaged. Any case, in these days of judo classes, women marathon winners, one supposes women can take care of themselves, or ought to be able to, and some can. Most can't. This one couldn't. If she could, she was delaying her counterattack until the oaf in the red jacket had worn himself out smacking her.

Bugger of it is, they shouldn't be obliged to take care of themselves, not against louts. That's my feeling, and if that's all it is, feeling, slop, laughably void of structured analysis, too bloody bad. She might've been a secret virago, she might've been the Manchester ladies' karate champion biding her time, the sight was still upsetting. She kept her eyes open. While her head was smacked to left and right, the eyes stayed on the redcoat's face. I stepped thitherwards, grabbed the slapping arm, and the back of a red collar, and jerked him away from her, half throttling him in the process, with luck.

He was all action, wheeling round and swinging a fist. But he was off balance, and held by his collar and one arm. I caught the whizzing fist and twisted it. While he was wondering what was going on I got his other wrist. Old Sergeant Loxton at training school would've been proud of me. Not that I'd ever been one of the stars.

Motivation, that's today's word. I can't see what's wrong with "passion," or "enthusiasm." Anyway, that's the secret of this kind of brush. No secret either. Feel strongly enough and you're off to a cracking start. We were face to face, panting somewhat. Being a lout, practiced in loutish ways, he's realised that if he struggled he could end up with two broken wrists, courtesy of a brother lout.

"Going it a bit, aren't you?" I said.

He said nothing. His eyes said it. Though his chin receded he couldn't have been described as a twi, a Bertie Wooster, Yankee-style. My grip had reduced him to a hunched, bent-knees posture. The girl had gone. She hadn't said where, or thank you, but she was right to go.

Now the chancy bit. I wasn't standing here all night holding this redcoat face-slapper. Any instant there'd be redcoats to the rescue. Same time, it'd been a while since I told anyone, "Promise to be good if I let you go?" Either I let him go or I broke his wrists.

I let him go and took a step back.

The choir was belting it out. Something about a Man with a Wheel.

I thought he was going to charge. I think he thought he was too. I'm still not sure why he didn't because that's dangerous wisdom about bullies being cowards. Still, I wasn't a girl. In fact he opened his mouth.

"You're a cop," he said.

"We say 'copper.' " One thing gets on my wick, it's being identified for what I am. It'd be the same if I were a doctor or road-mender. I feel I've failed somewhere, being told what I am.

"And I say you're off course—copper. Go flash your badge where it's needed."

"Like at the rest of you steward lot?"

"Like at Peter Ramsden, for a start."

"Who's Peter Ramsden?"

"Find out."

I think that's what he answered, but I'd been carrying on backing, step by step, glancing round at the turmoil, finding with one foot the step down from the emergency exit, so by then I wasn't hearing too well. If that was what he said, he was playing at push-button, television dialogue, because you don't name someone then say, "Find out," unless you're as mindless as the tough guy you're playing at being. He glared from afar. Other redcoats struggled with Trots and stevedores. The choir harmonised through the loudspeaker. Backing out of the hall, I was bumped and elbowed aside by Manchester's boys in blue streaming in. Carefully late they were, but not too obviously so, having dallied until all that might be required would be picking up the pieces.

The night was filthy. Sleet spat. For the first time in five minutes I remembered I was starving. Our 'Enry, far from home, and a wraith.

In these same moments, certainly not too many minutes later, the Tudor Inn must've been telephoning the hall to try and confirm with the Reverend James that it was in order, their admitting into his suite his press relations officer, Mr. Scott, a young man with a bruised face.

SEVEN

"I'm press relations for the Reverend James, your Coronet Suite, he's left his sermon there," I said, breathless. "Notes for his sermon, the one he's giving tonight. Terribly sorry. If you could let me have the key. Has he phoned you yet?"

My acting experience at university was useful for this impersonation of a press officer. At the same time, I wasn't acting being breathless. While I consider I'm passably fit, indeed athletic by comparison with most journalists, I'd just jogged three times round the Tudor Inn, a matter of about a mile in rain and snow.

It's these details which count. I might've forgotten the day of the week, or my own name, but I was hardly going to forget I was involving myself deeper and deeper with a murderer, someone who'd be unlikely to appreciate my interest. Naturally, I avoid clichés, but there are times when they serve, and when I say I knew I was playing with fire, that says it all. If I still didn't convince as a press officer who'd just hurtled from the Great Awakening rally, if there were house rules about keys, that was that. They weren't going to want a scene. The worst they could do would be to ask me to leave.

Worst or best. To be ruthlessly honest, I was so apprehensive I was rather hoping I wouldn't be given the keys to Jody James's room. I could've caught the next train back to London. I'd have done my best, and still have been intact.

The day had been pretty blank. Blank but worrisome,

awaiting this moment. I hadn't put in an appearance at home. I don't want to exaggerate the damage to my face, a couple of days and it'd heal, but mothers are mothers. One look and mine would've fainted.

The ten o'clock rendezvous in the foyer with the Reverend had been a swindle. I should've guessed. He and his retinue had left at nine for a tour of north country ruins. So I checked out of the Tudor Inn, parked my bag at the station, and spent the rest of the day smouldering.

I smouldered about the born-again circus in general, and in particular about Chinless the pug, the girl, who hadn't wasted any time telling Chinless I'd phoned her for a rendezvous, and the Reverend. Mostly about the Reverend. I know a fair amount about psychiatry, and clearly someone who combined murder with spreading the gospel of Christian love would be a psychopath, and surely paranoid. In the Reverend's case, dangerously so.

Where I smouldered was behind periodicals in the Central Library, the same library where in job-hunting days I'd listed forty-seven newspapers. I'd also smouldered at a matinée of an old spaghetti Western. At half past eight, when the rally ought to have reached intermission time, and I'd completed my ten-minute mile, and was looking the image of a press officer urgently dispatched by the Reverend James, I stood at the reception desk.

The day shift, who knew me as a battered ex-guest, had signed off. That was another vital detail. The evening shift didn't know me, and I didn't know them. I've watched Fleet Street hounds insinuate themselves past sentries and into sanctums on flimsier pretexts than being press officer for Jody James.

The girl in front of whom I was being breathless may've been matchlessly everything a lusty press officer could desire, but I wasn't observing. I was concentrating on my performance. I hadn't really expected her to hand over the key without ado, and she didn't. She consulted a superior in a black tie. No, sir, the Reverend James hadn't telephoned. What sermon might it be exactly, sir?

The one he was to be giving to a packed house any minute now. I looked at my watch a good deal. He'd left it

on the writing desk, he thought, the notes, or possibly by
the bed. Or in the cupboard. I kept pushing back my cuff
and regarding my Timex from the Eastleigh Woolworths—
still going strong, with the same scratched glass where it'd
grazed the esplanade seven years earlier. They could try
telephoning the Reverend James, that might be an idea,
but the difficulty was he'd be onstage praying. Waiting for
me to arrive with his sermon notes.

Another glance at the watch. I felt very much in control,
as you do when you're onstage. My acting out of these
details, such as the watch, was putting the wind up them.
Still the fellow hesitated. Come up with me if you've time,
I suggested. Shouldn't take long, not if we find the notes
right away.

That was a masterstroke. Certainly, it was a risk, but the
timorous who never dare to take a risk are those who're
left behind in life's race. The point was that a con man, a
suite rifler, would hardly invite the staff along as company. At the same time, doubt whether we'd ever lay our
hands on the miserable notes without sniffer dogs and
metal detectors might well deter a dutiful reception clerk
whose post was at reception. He nodded to the girl, who
invaded pigeonholes for the key to the Coronet Suite.

"I'm sure that'll be all right, sir. May I ask what name
it is?"

"Scott. C. P. Scott."

"You won't forget to return the key before you leave,
Mr. Scott?"

Feeling sorry for him, because if I were caught, if His
Pastorship found out and kicked up, the fellow was going
to be demoted to the kitchens, sink duty, I rode the lift
with the key in my hand and my hand in my pocket.

The corridor was empty. No one outside the door to the
Coronet Suite. I'd half expected redcoats. But they'd all be
at the rally, smashing demonstrators.

I listened at the door. The fatuity of what I was doing
finally came home.

The pointlesssness of the exercise had always been evident. I hadn't given it much thought because I'd never
imagined I'd get this far. What in the world did I suppose I

was going to find? A signed confession? "I, Jody C.
James, Founder and Minister of the First Born-Again Church
of God, do admit to having most foully murdered four
Middle Eastern gentlemen . . ." The truth was, I was
fairly desperate. Meeting the Reverend was becoming harder,
not easier. He was never alone, and to his bodyguard I was
now well known, a marked man in more senses than one.
In less than a week he and his whole BAGS shebang were
going to be back in the U.S.A., and at my current rate of
progress I'd have achieved nothing.

I found the light, closed the door behind me, and eyed
the airy spaces of a sitting room with flock wallpaper
bearing a coronet motif, reproduction Regency furniture,
and doors leading off. Though I hadn't cared to face it,
about all that was in my mind was plain, petty malice. Ink
over his Bibles. His clothes, papers, everything into the
bath, and turning on the taps. Seven years after the event
he was hardly likely to be leaving bloodstained burnouses
around. But at least I could get back at him for that punch
on the esplanade, and now for brushing me off like dan-
druff. "O vengeance," as someone said. Ideally, I'd have
been in the room of either Chinless, the bully, or Frizzy,
the betrayer, because I'd sooner have stuck a razor blade
in their soap than in Jody's.

I'm joking, of course. I'd never have gone that far.

Anyway, here I was. The Pastor's pad. The doors gave
onto a bedroom, a bathroom, and a minuscule kitchen. I
started with the bedroom. No Bibles, pictures of Jesus, or
framed photos of family. On the dressing table was a pile
of newspapers. Several *Posts*, one folded open at a story
of a Glasgow rally. By Peter Ramsden.

I discovered I was treading on tiptoe, then standing still,
listening, and feeling damp and hot. At least the bathroom
was only a short dash away. I opened a fitted cupboard,
dipped a hand through the pockets of dark suits, and felt
between and under columns of white shirts and underwear.
Among shoes and suitcases stood a rectangular red attaché
case. With contents, from the weight and rattle of it.
Locked.

In the kitchen sink, two unwashed cups. In the refrigera-

tor, butter, bananas, cans of beer. On an exiguous work
surface a jar of Canadian maple syrup, Lyle's Golden
Syrup, and a jumbo packet of Aunt Melinda's Buckwheat
Pancake Mix.

In the bathroom, shaving tackle, lotions, and pomades.
A jar of black pills, $4.25, from Moulton's Pharmacy,
West Third Street, Little Rock. Half hidden in the crab-
grass undergrowth of a bathmat, noticed by Hawkeye the
Newshound in spite of his preoccupation with nausea, a
hairpin.

The Reverend James didn't have enough hair to justify
hairpins. Plenty of his entourage did though. Another little
weakness, or a relic from earlier occupants of the Coronet
Suite? Given the standard of chambermaiding at the Tudor
Inn, probably it hadn't been there long. I let it be. It
wasn't the signed confession.

I stood straining to hear whether stewards might be
striding along the corridor. This wasn't cheeky sleuthing
for a gossip paragraph. This was broken legs country at the
very least. I could get out of it, out of this Coronet Suite,
and out of the BAGS campaign. Now, Helen with a
nonchalant wave would dismiss the affair. She'd be openly
in agreement on dropping it, utterly sympathetic, and from
her soapbox in the White Swan, among her rheumy-eyed
buddies, she'd be a sneering orator on the subject of the
insipid new generation of reporters.

In a corner cabinet in the sitting room stood Southern
Comfort, liqueurs for a sweet tooth, and a depleted Jim
Beam Bourbon which I further depleted with a lengthy pull
which left me spluttering. The stuff chased away the nausea instantly, which was as well because from a table by
the wall the telephone was ringing, and I was in no shape
to cope both with hot and cold flushes and the telephone.

Wrong number? A fan of the Reverend seeking salvation? Most likely it was reception eager to find out if I'd
discovered the sermon, in which case I should answer.

Another possibility was a steward routinely checking on
the holy of holies.

After watching for an unconscionable time the ringing
object, letting it ring, I went into action, opening drawers

in a chest, all empty, opening empty drawers in a taller chest, scurrying past veneered, empty coffee tables, searching armchairs and the carpet beside armchairs for the signed, ribbon-tied something that would reveal all, and aware of the phone's silence only when I'd completed the circuit and halted at the corner cabinet for a further *angst*-chasing swallow of good ol' Jim Beam.

All I came up with that was not impersonal, Tudor Inn furnishings was a Tudor Inn envelope with the Reverend's name on it, and "For Collection," and a stack of four or five paperbacks. The paperbacks were works of spiritual uplift or exegesis. One was Mortimer Adler's *How to Think About God*, which I'd not have thought proper reading for a fundamentalist because Adler, as far as I understood, rejected first causes and prime movers as presupposing the creator, and therefore begging the question. True, to promote fundamentalism you'd be better off knowing about natural causes, if only to be able to answer the hecklers. But were these paperbacks here to impress the chambermaid and bamboozle intruders from the *Post*, or was the Reverend James genuinely keen on religion?

The possibilities of the keys in the envelope didn't strike me at first. An accompanying note from the management informed the Reverend James that the handing out of pass keys did not accord with security policy. However, in view of the nature of the request, and the evident inconvenience should free access be denied for early morning prayer and intercession between the Minister and members of the Great Awakening Campaign team, as the management had been given to understand was the custom, in pursuance of the teaching of the First Born-Again Church of God, an exception would be made in full confidence that the Reverend James would be personally responsible for the safekeeping of the enclosed keys. The numbered disc attached to each key related, he would observe, to the floor on which the following rooms had been allotted to members of the Great Awakening . . .

Did Jody patrol from room to room raking BAGS sinners out of bed for prayer?

More probably he demanded free access to his team's

rooms to make sure no hanky-panky was going on. Or to
share in the hanky-panky. Whatever, the hotel hadn't been
going to fuss if the choice lay between handing over pass
keys and a cancelled block booking. If these spikey, basic-
looking bits of metal opened up so many doors, might they
do the trick for a red attaché case?

Back in the bedroom I hauled out the attaché case. I
prodded the locks with the pass keys. Not a hope. Useless.

There ought to have been something in the kitchen
which would force a lock. A knife, a tin opener. I headed,
with the attaché case, out of the bedroom and into the
kitchen, at which point a bell rang.

Not the telephone. Two brief buzzes. And again.

The door into the suite.

Now came lock and door-handle gratings, and after a
pause, knocking, and a voice. "Hello? Mr. Scott?"

I was a moment or two remembering who Mr. Scott
was. I put the two-pound tin of golden syrup into my
duffle-coat pocket and hurried out of the kitchen and into
the clerk in the black tie from reception. With him was a
fat little fellow, also in a black tie. The manager? Chair-
man of the board?

"Got it, the sermon—in the kitchen of all places!" I
cried, triumphant, holding aloft the attaché case, stepping past
them. "Must run!"

"We've been trying to telephone you, Mr. Scott. This
is—"

"The bath tap. Thought you should know. Leaking.
Needs a washer, wouldn't you think? Key's on the table.
Terribly grateful."

I loped from the Coronet Suite and along the corridor,
ignoring the lifts because there wasn't for ever for waiting
about. A leaky tap might hold them for five seconds. If
they hadn't liked the look of me, and I wouldn't have
liked the look of me, it might not.

Something kept them. When I glanced back from the
end of the corridor they were not in pursuit. Either they
were fitting a new washer or telephoning the foyer to have
me arrested. I ran down stairs to the floor below. With
more stately tread I advanced along the passage, past

familiar room numbers, and murmured, "Good evening," to an elderly couple filing by from the opposite direction. I passed my former room, scene of humiliation at the hands of Chinless. Too bad I didn't know his room number.

Petal Merchant's was one-two-eight.

Right here. According to the management's letter this floor needed key number three. I jiggled key number three fatuously, hopelessly, in the lock. The spikey finger of metal was like no key I'd ever seen. Possibly it might have worked for a locksmith. The door opened.

I stepped into the room and closed the door behind me.

I think at that time she was top on my malice list. Chinless was a straightforward bodyguard with fists who someday would meet someone with bigger fists. Jody-boy, well, retribution ultimately would gulp him, if not in this world, then in the next. But Pet Aversion?

A young, fetching singer with a job in a world of jobless. And a petty, paltry betraying bitch. All I'd done was suggest a cup of cocoa, and she'd bleated to guard-dog Chinless, who'd come scampering.

No Coronet Suite this. One room with bathroom off, exactly as I'd had, except here both beds would be taken, because Jody wasn't going to be paying for separate rooms when it was cheaper to share. I plucked back the cover of the nearest bed and under the pillow found a flimsy white nightie which told me nothing except that here, announced the tab in the collar, was 100 per cent polyester, warm machine or hand wash, cool iron. The pyjamas in the second bed were a mixture of polyester and cotton. A name tape revealed their owner as Roberta Kneeschorn.

So Petal's was the first bed. O rare deduction!

Carefully, I peeled back Petal's cover, blankets, and top sheet. An apple-pie bed would've been a jolly jape. The Golden Syrup, the lid of which I levered off with a ten-penny piece, was a jest of more mettlesome quality. Boys' reformatory school standard. Officers' quarters after the regimental dinner.

The tin was gratifyingly full. Upturned over the bed's approximate midpoint, it refused to release its too, too solid burden. Having progressed so far, this, I confess, was a dispiriting setback. I saw myself having to scoop out syrup with my fingers.

Then it descended. A slow, soundless cataract, yellowly gleaming, a sunlit hymn to sweetness, liquid amber upon hospital white. I could've signed my initials with it on the sheet.

I kept the stuff clear of the bed's upper reaches where she might have discovered it when she climbed in, but I allowed the lower area a frivolous squiggle for the fun of it. Life hadn't overflowed with the fun, the last day or two. The cataract became a rivulet, then a thread, then drips. Seeing no reason why sweetest Petal in her white polyester wouldn't slide her feet through the lake then settle her bottom in it, I geometrically reassembled the bed, neat as a nurse. I recouped the empty tin, its lid, and the attaché case, switched off the light, and left and locked the room.

Aiming for the stairs, after two strides I came to a stop. Someone heftily steward-sized had emerged round the end of the corridor and was advancing in my direction. Though he advanced saunteringly, and the chances were he'd be an unknown, unconcerned guest, heading bedward, I thought first of stewards. Then of management.

Money had been skimped on lighting the corridor. I resumed walking. Through opaqueness I saw no shine of redcoat cuff or lapel peeping from under the man's overcoat. And if he were management, why was he in overcoat and hat, carrying a paper bag in one had, in the other nourishment of some sort, which he lifted to his mouth and bit into? One of his shoelaces was undone and trailing. He audibly munched as he walked—munched or muttered, or hummed, or the three together. The rich, slightly squelchy sounds he was making weren't easy to identify, but I had the impression of someone at the end of a gruelling Lenten fast, though we weren't in Lent. By the time we'd drawn close my interest had waned to a point where I no longer needed to study him, because what mattered was whether he was a steward, or management, and obviously he wasn't either. All I knew was that I didn't know him, and if I didn't shift I'd miss my train to London.

Just the same, even if he hadn't accosted me, even if we hadn't met again, three thousand miles from the Tudor Inn, under harrowing circumstance, I'm sure I'd have remembered him. Some individuals simply happen to leave a print, and this was one. After all, he was fairly bizarre, I thought, with his hat worn indoors, the trailing shoelace, and in his hand what I identified as a meat pie.

Accosted, I should add, isn't perhaps the precise word. He'd stopped. He'd even stopped munching. But he failed to stop me. When, as I walked by, I glanced at him, he was regarding me with interest, as if it were I who might be the management, or the Fattest Lady in the World.

"Excuse me," he said, very indistinctly from swallowing and packed hamster's cheeks.

I grunted an all-purpose grunt and trod faster along the corridor.

"Ramsden?" he called after me with a rising inflexion. Bits of pie must have sprayed through the air. "Peter Ramsden?"

He was too late, whoever he was. Lovely to be known, to be famous, but I'd reached the end of the passage. Once round the corner I galloped.

On a step of the stairs I deposited the empty syrup tin. Unimpeded, I hastened through the foyer. In the forecourt, wordlessly as I passed him, I handed the envelope of pass keys to the commissionaire with the Cromwellian wart, not caring whether he remembered me or not.

What would it matter? The management, stewards, the police even, now I was an attaché-case thief, none of these would've needed to be masterminds to discover who'd been horsing around at the Tudor Inn. I'd burned enough bridges to warm a colony of Eskimos, and for nothing, if nothing was what the attaché case held.

EIGHT

"What have we here?" said I with my mouth full. "Goose? Moose? I spy aubergine. Moose moussaka? Elk?"

"Smaller."

"Goat?"

"Keep trying."

"Stoat?"

"Close. Ferret."

"Timbale of ferret. A miracle."

I forked home more timbale, if that's what it was, which whatever it was was piquant enough to have played havoc with the stomachs of Miriam's frailer archaeologists, those who, daring to the very rim of madness, might've chanced it in place of the steamed cod.

They're a perk, we've never considered it stealing, these leftovers Miriam brings home. Usually they're leftover leftovers, the end of the line even for archaeologists with their minds on shards. They've already done service as a roast, then cold cuts, than a fricassee, before becoming this mashed, macerated, massacred, possibly even masticated, but valiantly jazzy, aubergine-enriched compost from the *prix fixe*.

"And then what?" she demanded, wanting more, or the same over again, perversely enjoying her anger. "Was it all hate? Didn't he even try to justify the creation, Adam and Eve, all that?"

"How d'you mean, justify?"

"Proofs, scientific evidence, simple reason. I don't know. Astronomy. Anything. He's got to offer something apart from the Bible."

"Why? The Bible's it. He doesn't need anything else."

"He'd have needed something else if I'd been there!"

"Exactly. You weren't there. He's holding spiritual pep rallies, not theological seminars. More political than spiritual, if you ask me. Still, he's preaching to the converted."

"Except for the protestors."

"Right. Except for the protestors."

The *Post* had carried only a paragraph on the fisticuffs in Manchester. No policeman having been felled, and this policeman's less than sensational brush with a redcoat having gone unrecorded by the cameras, the story obviously hadn't been thought to amount to much. Peter Ramsden's by-line had been absent.

I'd got back to London after a side trip to Bradford, which hadn't been a waste of time, amazingly, because the police had lined up for me relatives claiming to be relatives of my Bahawalpurans. Back at the Factory I'd spent an hour mixing immigration paper work with a couple of born-again calls. Now was timbale time, watched by Miriam, very beautiful and cross in her boy's boarding-school dressing gown, a weighty, scratchy, tartan garment with a tasselled cord.

"Did you know," she wanted to know, "that in the States they've got to teach creationism in the schools? Some schools anyway. There've been court cases. It's spreading and getting worse. If they teach evolution they've got to balance it with creationism, otherwise it's a violation of religious liberty. They're censoring and doctoring science books."

She was cross with the Book of Genesis, not with me, or not yet, though I'd returned without having had the Reverend James annulled and shipped back to the boondocks, if that's the word. I know Little Rock's not the boondocks, or I was guessing it wasn't, but you don't learn to become a primitive, a fundamentalist rabble-rouser, in the city. Do you? Presumably he'd arrived there from one of those swamps where they wind rattlesnakes round their necks and burn crosses and blacks.

It's complicated though, like gold flow, and bending spoons. There must be plenty of people who accept the

Bible as literal truth who're shy and unfanatical. Just as there're fanatics who foam about superstition at the drop of the name Jesus. Now there're biologists saying Darwin got it wrong, or at any rate not wholly right, because evolution isn't slow, continuous change, it's sudden bursts of change after millions of years of nothing, so if the polar bear happened suddenly, why not the world? And if the evolutionary process is abrupt leaps, revolutionary leaps, that's handy for Marxists looking for a boost from science.

At the end of the day, which this was, thank God, tricky stuff for a working policeman with enough problems trying to master the new immigration laws. I wasn't in much of a mood for talking about it.

Miriam was. Her day had been divided between household instructions for smoking Sigrid, the *au pair*, cooking for the archaeologists, and dandling Sam, who's a winner in many respects but wouldn't be your first choice for the interchange of ideas.

"It's a fad," I told her, wiping my plate with bread. "Delicious. What's the main course?"

"What's a fad?"

"A pet notion. Something that doesn't last. A fashion—"

"I know what a fad is. What fad are you talking about?"

"These creationists. Nothing new. They've always been there, lurking. They're best ignored."

"Like the gas chambers, you mean? Weren't they a fad? Attila, you could call him a fad. Genghis Khan. I mean, they all go away in the end, they don't last. The Red Brigade. Black Thursday. White Friday. The PLO. IRA. Baader Meinhoff." Her cheeks were pinkening. Miriam writes letters for Amnesty. She gets very distressed. "Hijackers, kidnappers, pushers, Amin, Bokassa, Pinochet, Jack the Ripper, footpads, skinheads, punks—"

"Hold on. Jesus! This is beginning to sound like Jody James. For a start, punks may dye themselves orange and lilac—"

"I don't care about punks, I care—"

"You brought up punks, not me."

"If you took these born-again monsters seriously and wasted less—"

"I take them seriously. I'm seeing one tomorrow. I'll be surprised if he's a monster."

There'd been a memo on my desk. Someone claiming to be one of the Reverend James's road show had been telephoning wanting a word with our God Squad, which, as I've said, we don't have.

Didn't have. Because I'd visited the Manchester rally, and because the rest of the CID, all three thousand of them, had reasons for having nothing to do with it, we'd got one now, unofficially and part-time.

I'd phoned the number in the memo, which was the Hilton, but he hadn't wanted to meet there, so we were going too meet opposite, in the snow. He hadn't given anything away, apart from an American accent. I couldn't guess whether he wanted to hand over the balance sheet or try to convert me. The other possibility was he was the face-slapper, the rough one who'd thought I should be flashing my badge at Peter Ramsden, and he'd be waiting with reinforcements and snowballs. Whatever, it wasn't going to be more than thirty minutes out of the day.

I took them seriously, the born-again lot, but I may have misled Miriam in telling her as much, because I didn't take them all that seriously, certainly not from a police point of view. What after all was happening at these rallies? A blameless crowd of believers, and predictable punch-ups which the stewards had been competent to cope with.

My interest was holding up though. For one thing, I'd seen the Reverend live onstage, and though I'd not want to repeat the experience, it hadn't been totally boring.

For another, I got irritated by unfinished business, loose ends, if you like, which is barmy because half the time in police work there's nothing else. I'd had more than twenty years to get used to the pattern of opening a file, watching it wax, then wane, and finally moulder on the shelf, open and incomplete, awaiting the inspired guess, or tip-off, or confession. Ramsden, for instance, whom I'd hoped to see and hadn't, he was a loose end. How were his legs and where was he?

Fact was, though I could hardly tell Miriam, my interest had shifted somewhat from the Reverend to the reporter.

The redcoat bloke had known Ramsden, or known about him. What about him? Why Ramsden, and not someone on the *Sun*, or *The Times?* What was it to the red-coated, horrible face-slapper whether I flashed my badge at Ramsden or not? Not that it hadn't crossed my mind that if I knew more about Ramsden, I might learn more about the Reverend. If whatever I might learn about the Reverend was discreditable, something the Home Office could hammer him with, Miriam would be over the moon. I'd get an extra egg for breakfast.

Had that been Ramsden in the corridor at the Tudor Inn, the bruised young man with the red attaché case who'd failed to answer to the name Ramsden? Failed to answer but skedaddled off sharpish.

That corridor had been not only mine but several of the BAGS party's, and Ramsden's too, before he'd checked out. But he'd checked out, so what was he doing there ten hours later? Why wasn't he covering the rally? The *Post* had said he'd be covering it.

I've got mates to whom these kinds of questions are a joy and a challenge. To me, often as not, they're so much sand in the skull. On the other hand, these itched like sand, for no reason I could think of. This batch I was resolved to dispose of tomorrow. What matter if I'd missed Ramsden up north? I'd see him here. Fleet Street was no farther from the Yard than Hyde Park.

That'd leave an uncluttered head and a clear evening for telly with Miriam, or a pint at the Anchor, or our local Screen on the Green, so long as it wasn't Ingmar Bergman or Woody Allen. Alternatively, there was always gin rummy with Sam, who eats the cards. Miriam could choose. If the muse were agreeable I might dash off a *villanelle*.

Plenty of rhymes for Jody James. Toady dames . . . hell's flames . . . throw the bugger in the Thames . . .

"Who?" Miriam said.

"Sorry?"

"The one you're seeing tomorrow."

"Called himself French, or Finch."

"Not James? His Most Turned-Around Reverency, His Divine Fundament—?"

She cocked her head, listening. She rarely hears when I propose we open a third bottle of wine, but some sounds she'd hear halfway round the world.

"I'll get him," I said, sliding out of my chair. "You change him. Fair?"

First point I noticed about my customer from the road show was that he was black. Kiss me Hardy, my powers of observation were sharp that morning!

Second, his were sharper. When I spotted him he was standing bareheaded in a dark overcoat and scarf by the bench, watching me. True, there was no one else to watch, but in the instant I saw him he gestured to me. That was weird because we'd never met, he couldn't have recognized me. I remember being so disoriented as to believe, momentarily, I was not God Squad but Illegal Immigration, and here was an illegal immigrant waiting by appointment with his dicey, crumpled documents and a very long story.

Third, his voice.

"Chief Inspector Peckover?"

It was almost too much. Paul Robeson with a *soupçon* of Harry Belafonte. You'd have described it as rich if you'd liked him, fruity if you didn't. He'd taken off a glove and was extending his hand, which I shook.

I said, "Mr. French?"

"Glad to know you."

"Not Finch?"

"I don't believe so."

He didn't believe so. Now he should've asked if I were doubting his name was French, but he didn't. He stood there wearing a polite smile, sprouting icicles, waiting for me to explain, if I chose to.

Fourth thing then, he had coolth.

He'd have been thirtyish. He didn't have the height of Lemonhead Chamberlain or Wilt the Stilt—I've got the names wrong but you know who—but he was no gnome.

I said, "What can I do for you?"

"Walk." The monosyllable throbbed like a double-bass string. "Else we're both into a pneumonia situation. It's as much as what I can do for you, Chief Inspector. Like recommending you keep an eye on this newsman, Ramsden.''

''Flash my badge at him?''

''Sir?''

''I don't have a badge. Got a warrant card, but no one ever gave me a badge. I'll look into the badge situation. If I don't look into Ramsden, is he going to get his legs broken?''

''Something like that,'' he said, walking fast. ''You don't need telling, you're a policeman, sir, and I'm talking routine law and order. It'd be bad publicity for our church, any serious trouble. Simply, we'd appreciate it if you were aware of this young man. If he's aware of you, so much the better. Maybe he'll lay off.'' Striding along the soggy path, he punched his gloved fists together as if trying to warm them. ''He's got his knife in us. He's not alone. The pinko long-hairs, the me-generation wasters and atheists, we like to think we're gaining ground, our church, but we run up against them all the time, the troublemakers. People like Ramsden. Problem is, sir, there are some in our church who're not pacifists. You understand?''

''Badly.''

''You get a church with real crusading faith, there'll be plenty ready to fight back. Tooth and claw, Chief Inspector. They'd be doing the Lord's will.''

They or we? Was he including himself among those who'd break legs to defend the true and only fundamentalist faith?

Shoes squelching, breath pumping, we trod along a path parallel with the traffic in Park Lane. There was nothing so picturesque as snow, only rain, which was beginning to fill the brim of my hat. A sprig of foil-wrapped heather had arrived from Willie Smith in Glasgow—more a clump than a sprig, about ten inches of it—and I was going to keep it in my hatband until Scotland won the World Cup.

Dismal empty park stretched away in the murk. Through the trees to our left, beyond the flooding traffic, loomed a choice of the West End's multistarred hotels, grandiose constructions from between the wars, or in one or two instances from barely yesterday.

"That's all, sir, I've said, it," he said, though he continued walking. "I'd like to think I'm being alarmist, but why take chances? Maybe he thinks he's doing his job, but I'm sorry, Ramsden's become a dirty word among some of our members. A suggestion in his editor's ear, would that do it? It'd come better from you than us. Could be you'd be saving yourself a stack of trouble. Saving everyone trouble, most of all our zealous newshound. You Britishers are champions at the grapevine game, the school-tie network, am I right? 'Suggest you offer Carruthers a spot of time off, old bean. Ticket to the Pongo-Pongo Hill Station, what? Hush-hush, under your hat, by Jove?' If he could be kept off our necks until we fly out, sir. It's only another three days."

"Figuring we jest might lock him in the hoosegow till the lynch mob's shaken the dust, that what you're figuring?" I glanced sideways. Soddit, he was unamused. I thought I'd been fairly funny. He might even have been weeping, or it might've been rain. "Are you telling me this in a private capacity, or as the Reverend James's personal emissary?"

"Something like that."

We halted at the railing along Serpentine Road. Beyond leafless trees, beyond dingy, sodden grass, the traffic swarmed round Hyde Park Corner.

"Something like that," I echoed. "If your Reverend James was happy for you to talk to the police we'd not be here in a pneumonia situation. We'd be in the Hilton. Coffee and doughnuts. The full public gaze. Waste of breath asking you questions, seems to me, but here're a few anyway. Why's Ramsden a dirty word with your lot? What makes you think he's got his knife in you? Have his stories been any different from the rest of the press? Are you trying to involve the police with everyone who fails to love your church? What's special about Ramsden?"

I wasn't expecting or waiting for answers, but he was listening. We'd started back along the path.

"What's special," I told him, sidestepping a puddle, "is he knows something about you that others don't. Not religion, or politics either. That's so thin you disappoint

me. Money?'' I paused, offering him the chance to confirm
or deny. Nothing. ''Where's the loot go that you collect
from your converts? Guns for the creationist revolution?''

I'd only just thought of that. Sounded a bit lame.

Sounded preposterous.

Money though. Money for high living and silk suits?
Votes for Jody, next president of the U.S.A.?

I wasn't entirely on the wrong track with money. Money
had been the reason why four Arabs went over the cliff at
Pithley. But I didn't know it then. The Arabs never entered
my head. Where I was wholly off the track was thinking
Ramsden was interested in the born-again church generally, not its Reverend James specifically.

''What trouble if he's not kept off your necks?'' I was
getting annoyed. ''He's not on you necks. He wasn't even
at your last rally. You'll probably never hear of him
again. He's not even in the office today. He'll be somewhere like Yarmouth fabricating the great bloater scandal.''

That wasn't true about Yarmouth. I'd tried to reach
Ramsden at the *Post* but it was his day off, so they'd said.
After a fair amount of debate they gave me his home
number, you'd have thought they'd been parting with their
next six exclusives, but he hadn't been at his flat either. In
lieu of Ramsden I'd won a grudging rendezvous with
Helen Goodenough. Later, in a pub. She'd sounded pretty
offhand. I'd know her by her Rothmans King Size carrying
the government warning. There was no guarantee she was
going to be better than nothing.

''Wherever Yarmouth is, he should stay there,'' the
BAGS man said.

''Gawd, back to the leg-breaking. Have you listened to
a word? Unless you can offer something a little more solid
than Ramsden not being passionate for your church, there's
nothing I can do.''

''We've reason to believe,'' he said, bass string twanging through the murk, ''that Ramsden continues to be
maliciously interested in our church to a degree threatening
a breach of the peace.''

The familiarity of that sort of language might've brought

me to a stop if we'd not already come to one, by the bench where we'd met. He was removing a glove.

He said, "You keep on about legs, sir. I thought I'd been clear, legs are nowhere. He could go permanently missing."

"What," I said, "has he actually done?"

"Tampered," he said with a vague gesture.

Tampered. Terrific. The bloke's black eyelids drooped indicating this was close-down, I could make what I would of "tampered."

"So what in fact's your name?" I said.

"Foster."

"I've seen you, second or third from the end, right-hand side. Baritone?"

"Bass."

His name might've been Foster, I could look him up in the press kit. If it were, he was trusting me more than he'd trusted his BAGS mates. Why leave a false name with the Yard unless it was to protect himself against complications if we phoned back? Such as another singer taking the call, or his name being paged for all the hotel plus the Reverend to hear.

I said, "And you saw me?"

"The press table. Fidgeting."

"You thought I was press?"

"I didn't think anything, sir. You blew when the fighting started, almost. Found yourself a private war. That was our chief steward."

"He thought I should do something about Ramsden too."

"Sure he did. We all do. If everyone kept his distance, cultivated his own garden, everything would stay nice and peaceful. But Ramsden's screwing it up. Look at it this way, like a triangle, pee-one, two, and three. Our church represented by our pastor, you the police, Ramsden the press. Ramsden's going to collapse that triangle. He's already sucked in you, the law. So open a lawbook, sir. Put him on ice till we've gone home. You'll think of something you can hold him for."

"Bad spelling?"

"He's got a fancy car. Where's he get the money?"

"Are you a copper?" I said.

"That's wild. I'm a singer."

I don't know why we shook hands, unless it was because his glove was off. The vibes were a mix of respect,
suspicion, curiosity, and boredom, cancelling each other
out and leaving only reverberating bass strings in a void
like the black hole which may have been the beginning of
creation, though not in the opinion of the First Born-Again
Church of God. I didn't stand watching him walk away
into the enveloping grey like a character in a John le Carré
book either, though I suppose I might've done if it hadn't
been so bloody cold.

He squelched Hiltonwards. Soaked, sodding Buggins
splashed along a more southerly route, there being cheaper
beer at the Rose and Crown in Old Park Lane.

The White Swan off Fleet Street had reasonable beer
too. I'd never been there before. London has about seventeen million pubs and I'm not a collector. This one would've
been known to the locals as the Mucky Duck because
White Swans usually are, and it was crammed. Journalists
presumably. Printers, delivery men. Possibly an escaped
lawyer or two from down the road, though seven o'clock
was late for lawyers.

"Miss Goodenough?" I lifted and lowered my hat.

On the mat by her glass were Rothmans King Size. She
was already signalling to the barmaid.

"What'll you have?" she said in a remembered soda-
syphon voice.

Somebody else identifying me as a plainclothes plod.
We'd never met. For all she knew I might've been a
yachting correspondent in search of a job. On the other
hand, this was the time and the place, and she might've
looked me up in the cuttings. My matchless Adonis features have illumined the pages of the public prints once or
twice.

Adonis and Aphrodite. She might've been Aphrodite
once, it was hard to tell, not least because visibility through
the smoke was down to centimetres. If she'd been a beauty,

it'd gone. Her eyes were damp and pouchy, she wore a necklace of what might've been opals—are they the unlucky ones?—and her figure was conical, what you could see of it. Under a fur coat which hung open she had on a knitted wool dress that looked decently classical. Not that I'd know. She was lighting a cigarette from the butt of the old and sat on a high stool at the end of the bar, her back against the wall. Since fifty other customers probably wouldn't have said no to the stool, either she'd occupied it since opening time or it was hers by some ancient law of Mucky Duck stool tenure.

"Och aye," she said, regarding my hat with its flourishing clump of heather.

"These born-again Americans," I said. "What d'you think? Have you been? Watched them in action?"

"I covered Billy Graham at Wembley twenty years ago."

"Seen one, seen 'em all?"

"I go home evenings. Too much lawlessness on the streets." She slid a five-pound note across the counter towards the barmaid. "Is that what you want to talk about—religion?"

"What're they doing here? You should know about trends, if that's what they are. Finger on the pulse. Must've cost them a penny, and they don't seem to be getting any more publicity than a fourth-division football match. Good health." A pint had arrived, and for Madam, gin. "Mean, why here? Is everyone in the States already converted?"

"Kudos." She was expert in directing her smoke away from me, sometimes downward through her nose, sometimes by turning her head, and sometimes by compressing and so contorting her mouth as to create at one corner an orifice through which jetted, at a tangent, the exhaled stream. "It's nothing to do with money, not directly. They go home with an international track record. The Born-Again Hootenanny fresh from its unbelievable triumph in Great Britain with standing ovations from the Queen and Royal Family, Paul McCartney, Julie Andrews, Alistair Cooke, Peter O'Toole, Margaret Thatcher, that lad who won the gold for ice skating—who else do we have Americans have heard of?''

"I thought she'd named them all. "Kim Philby?" I offered. "Ronald Biggs?"

"A Las Vegas comic's made it internationally when he walks onstage at the Palladium, unless I'm out of date." She tipped a driblet of tonic into her gin. "John McEnroe needs Wimbledon. Jody James needs the Albert Hall."

Her eyes looked beyond me, seeking cronies in the crush. Here was her home, here with booze, fags, and fellow scribblers, buddies from forgotten campaigns, forecasting together tomorrow's splash, swapping the day's slanders and unprintable rumours, and reliving battles long ago, the foreign uprisings and *coups d'état,* plane and train crashes, volcanoes erupting far away, bombings across the Irish Sea, scandals, summits, murders, and best of all, the nights with hip flask and chequebook on the doorstep of the balding, sixty-year-old Earl of Twirl, head of MI66, Nobel prizewinner, godfather to royalty, run to earth and believed shacking up then and there behind the Georgian panelled door, the damask curtains, with pert, petite, East German starlet and KGB operative Hilde Schmilde, aged fourteen.

"Whatever you've got on them, if it's criminal"—I sought her eyes through the smoke—"if it's liable to lead to any sort of aggro, before they clear off home, you should speak up, you'd be doing yourself a favour. You be fair with us, we'll be fair with you." Gor, the banality! The same words exactly that used to be fed us, nonstop, as cadets, and in the army. "Whatever you say, money comes into it. Money always comes into it. They swan into Britain, pray, pass the hat round, and skip out with the booty. A million-dollar con job. I'll be frank, we know what's going on. The Fraud Squad's onto it. Don't quote me."

"Sorry?"

"Sorry you know nothing, or sorry you're not saying?"

"Sorry, you've lost me."

She can't have been too enamoured of me, I was probably ruining her evening, but she was making a fair fist of hiding it. In her trade you never knew when one good turn might pay off. When the friendly acquaintance of a CID officer might come in.

Mutual, of course. But day to day we need them less than they need us.

"So what's the *Post*'s interest?" I said.

"What interest? Normal reader interest. Sorry, dear, I really don't understand. If there's a story, we print it. If there isn't, we don't."

"You've got a reporter covering them full-time. Or you had. There was a threat to break his legs."

"Please. An army colonel in Beirut once threatened me with consequences that'd make even your hair curl."

"Why didn't Ramsden cover the Manchester rally?"

"Ill. Fell in his bath. Smashed in every sense, so I'd imagine. But not, I gather, his legs. An act of God and excess."

"Does he own a red attaché case?"

"Good heavens, how'd I know?"

"Will he cover the grand finale?"

"What grand finale?"

"Tomorrow. The Albert Hall."

"That's a reasonable question. Your first. Answer, couldn't tell you. What's it matter? If he doesn't go, someone else will, unless real news breaks." She gestured to the barmaid. I dug in my pocket. I'd be skint in a week if this kept up. "He should have, would have, but he's got at least three days off owing. He said he'd take them now if he weren't needed, which he isn't."

"What's he do with his days off?"

"Not the faintest idea. He has girl friends, a car."

"Nice car?"

Something foreign, I think. A Saab? Third-hand. It's always in some garage waiting for new parts. Could be fourth-hand."

"Who're the girl friends?"

"They're fourth-hand. He diverts us with their history from time to time. We were quite impressed by his account of nights with a certain actress whose name may

have swum across your ken, but Peter likes to impress.
You don't necessarily believe him.''

"Why would you? He's a newspaper reporter.''

"What makes you think so?''

"Are you saying he's no good?''

"Impossible to tell, dear. The *Post* isn't a newspaper,
it's exclamation marks and breasts. Let me know if ever
you find a story in it more than five lines long. It'll mean
we're slipping.''

"What's an exclusive worth to a reporter? A big exclusive? Does he get his salary doubled?''

"Heavens, no.'' She was signalling again to the barmaid. As her glass was half full I assumed she was beginning to hoard for the winter. "Depends. For a week or two
his expenses wouldn't be queried. Within reason. Is it the
born-again lot you're investigating, or Peter?''

"I'm asking you nothing I wouldn't ask him. You don't
have to feel disloyal.''

"I'll try not to.'' She asked the barmaid for cigarettes,
shifted her bottom on the bar stool, waved to a chum in the
throng, drank, and said, "Peter would like to be doing our
gossip column—''

"Thought your whole paper was a gossip column.''

"—because he believes that'd give him a cachet in
society.'' She ignored the interruption. She was blowsy,
boozy, catty, tough, bright, very feminine, and, I guessed,
dependable to the death, if need be. "Peter sees himself as
a frustrated highbrow. He's as highbrow as a battery hen.
He considers himself too good for the *Post*, he thinks he
should be on *The Times*. Poor boy, he'll probably grow up,
though he's taking his time. The truth is, we're all too
good for the *Post*. He's not special. Have I said anything I
shouldn't? There's no real harm in Peter. He's overpaid
and almost certainly undersexed. I'd hazard you'll be vice
versa, though that heather, really, it does nothing for you.
Did you get it at a sex shop?'' She was simultaneously
swallowing gin, blowing smoke, and laughing. "Why don't
you send us some poems? Keep them to five lines. You
never know. We've never run a poem. God knows what
we'd pay. Far too much. Peter'd spit, he'd be so jealous.''

So, she'd looked me up in the cuttings. "Jealous about the money," I asked, "or the poem?"

"Both, dear. Especially the money."

"O take the cash, and let the cachet go."

"I wouldn't be surprised."

"Is he hard up?"

"Darling, who isn't?" Helen Goodenough stubbed out her cigarette. "I never said this, but he may have a problem with Desmond's Club."

"Berkeley Square?"

"No idea."

"How much?"

"Ask Peter, don't ask me."

"He's not at his flat."

"Keep trying. He phoned in an hour ago." She lit a cigarette. "I assumed he was phoning from there, but I suppose he could've been anywhere."

"Why'd he phone?"

"See if anything was doing."

"On his day off?"

"He's keen. Don't policemen ever phone in on their days off?"

"If they're keen." When they had a day off. Life with Illegal Immigration was a doodle, but I remember in Vice four months without a day off. "Was anything doing?"

She appeared to reflect. Her powdered cheeks bulged, exhalation being imminent. If she chose, I was going to get it between the eyes.

"The born-again man, Jody James, he'd telephoned offering Peter an interview," she said. The smoke was travelling for the most part over my left shoulder. "Don't ask me when or where, I don't know. If there is an interview, they'll arrange it themselves."

"You don't like Ramsden, do you?"

She didn't answer that one, which was answer enough. I bought her a double Gordon's before raising my hat and leaving.

Her Majesty's Gaming Board inspectors, the courts, and the press, *Private Eye* mainly, have been giving our West

End gambling clubs a bumpy ride recently. Some of the clubs. So they're nervous, they're on their best Sunday behaviour. High time too.

I'm not saying Desmond's welcomed me with instant honorary membership and a box of complimentary chips, but they didn't throw me out, which they'd have been entitled to do. The secretary was a Mr. Ronnie somebody who didn't risk jokes, like asking which sex shop my lucky heather came from, but insinuated me into his office before the nostrils of the punters could be polluted by the whiff of a plod. He offered Cognac, and out of a box file plucked the Ramsden dossier, which was one sheet of foolscap showing losses totalling £1,200, and signatures. Compared with the bad debts of certain celebrities and moneybags Ronnie was happy to name, Ramsden was birdseed, his owings the result of bad club management and it all having happened so quickly. Yes, Ronnie agreed, once upon a time a couple of heavies would've visited him, but not today, thanks very much, not with all the interest. Though maybe tomorrow. Depended. Imponderables. Things would quieten down, and twelve hundred was twelve hundred, plus interest of the twenty per cent variety, minimum.

Moderately worried, Ronnie explained that whatever the police concern might be, and he wasn't asking, if Ramsden didn't fetch up in prison, so much the better, prisons being the one place the club would probably have to write him off, so far as recouping went, though not for putting the boot in.

I was in and out of Desmond's in eight minutes flat, thereabouts.

NINE

No question about it, this was cathedrals week. Three days earlier, Manchester Cathedral. Now St. Paul's.

Neither had been of my choosing. Given the choice, I'd have had them bottom of my list, this time of year. If *The Times* had offered me tomorrow the job of church affairs reporter I'd have turned it down. I'd have had to, because of the sub-zero temperatures in cathedrals. Presumably an ecclesiastic correspondent would need to spend at least some of his time in cathedrals.

I believe I am by nature quite a detached person, as of course an impartial reporter ought to be, but in spite of the refrigerated air, I smouldered once again. People talk about "cold fury." I don't know, perhaps some people go cold with fury. I go tropical. If I'd taken my shoes and socks off, my toes would've been smoking like liquid nitrogen.

Stymied by redcoats from meeting His Pastorship in Manchester Cathedral. Now not meeting him again, because he wasn't here.

A few frozen sightseers with guidebooks were here. In the pews still fewer meditated, not that they're pews in St. Paul's, they're chairs, as the world must know after That Wedding. But the Reverend had proposed the time as well as the place, I'd arrived on time, my watch said ten-thirty, and I'd been waiting half an hour.

He might've been battling through the traffic. The Hilton was a fair distance. He might've been down in the crypt with the long dead, contemplating the bust of George

Washington. Or up in the dome whispering warnings about fornication to the other side of the Whispering Gallery.

Fools never learn. This was the Tudor Inn over again—"Ten o'clock in the lobby tomorrow morning, Mr. Ramsden.". The difference was that this time he'd sought me out. He'd telephoned me at home at the moment I was having my ego comforted by April, a frolicsome baggage from the *Post*'s classified ads, with whom naturally I have nothing in common, other than country matters.

"Ten o'clock at St. Paul's tomorrow morning, Peter."

That was another difference. Now it was Peter. He'd suggested this spot near the lectern, at the corner of the choir and north transept, by the bust of Dr. Johnson. His instructions had started vaguely and ended precisely, as if he'd been studying a plan.

A one-time chauffeur and guide for religious tours might well have had cathedral booklets to hand. He might've stood on this same arctic spot showing Dr. Johnson off to tourists.

Why he'd sought me out was a question I'd hoped would be answered when we met here. Certainly his intention was not to honour me with a horse's mouth account of his church. He must've suffered desperate delusions of grandeur if he supposed the *Post* cared. Give an exclusive interview to the *Post* or any other paper today, moreover, and come tomorrow's press conference the rest of the press would stay away in droves. He'd have known that.

A young cleric in a black gown scuttled past without a glance, into the ambulatory. Why were minor officials in cathedrals always in a hurry?

Probably trying to keep warm.

Ten thirty-five. I stamped my feet, fretted, fumed. I'd give him another five minutes, maximum.

Fourth time, was it, or the fifth, I'd made that decision?

Here anyway was the spot. Jody in his courier days had never shown Dr. Johnson off to tourists, or if he had he'd had his eyes shut, because it wasn't a bust, it was a statue on a great block of marble, imperious in Roman toga, very muscular, his brainy head on his fist, incubating apothegms. *Samveli Iohnson*.

I have always been a devotee of the Doctor. "He was a very good hater." That was Dr. Johnson.

Jody as chauffeur and courier may not have observed Johnson, but Johnson had got Jody's number. Jody was an excellent hater of communists, abortionists, homosexualists . . .

"He is no wise man that will quit a certainty for an uncertainty."

That too, I was fairly sure, stamping, blowing into cupped hands, watching the aisle, was Johnson. He ought to have been talking about betting when he said that, but he was talking about me. To me, if you like. The certainty was Jody James was a killer, and with luck, one day, headlines. My headlines. For me to back out now would be to return to the uncertainty of every other piddling news item of the day, the months, the lengthening years. All the rubbish, all the potty ephemera.

So hang in, *mon vieux*. Until eleven, anyway. Hope springs eternal. Bastard Reverend. Then to the Hilton to pour treacle in his bed. Scorpions in his shoes. Brimstone on his toothbrush. The shocking part of this was that I meant it. I was sweaty from a vindictiveness which must always have been there, without my knowing, and had surfaced since the Reverend came to town. If my imagination hadn't been frozen solid I'd have hatched grimmer nastiness. Like that horse's head in somebody's bed in *The Godfather*. The horse had been a favourite, that was the point. So what was a favourite of His Pastorship that could go under his pillow? His organist's finger?

Quite likely Jody hated his organist. He'd probably have been delighted.

Money? One place to hurt Jody would be his purse.

All puerile, sweaty fantasy. I didn't see myself looting the BAGS coffers because I wouldn't have known where to begin. Finance has never been among my stronger points. There'd be bank accounts, numbered ones in the Cayman Islands. He hadn't kept the church funds in his attaché case.

It was freezing! My day off too, I could've been in bed, I could've been telephoning April, warming her up for a night of romance, after the Albert Hall. The gowned cleric, or another gowned cleric, scampered out of the ambulatory carrying a clipboard.

In the red attaché case Jody had kept mainly BAGS papers. Itineraries, schedules, invoices, press clippings on his television appearance, airline tickets. There'd been an unused chequebook for a personal account at a Little Rock branch of the First National City Bank, and his passport, greenish and new, signed by "I, the undersigned Secretary of State . . . Alexander Haig," which failed to show that seven years earlier Jody James had entered Britain, whether or not he'd been using that name at the time. There'd also been a little box which should've held cuff links, or a wedding ring, but contained a dental plate with wire and a solitary tooth, the top left incisor, though I'm not a dentist.

Much good it'd do me. To have challenged Jody-boy with his false tooth might've been to risk a terminal trip to Pithley, or similar. He wasn't going to offer instant remorse and a confession.

Still, somehow he'd have reacted. He'd surely have talked if only to deny everything, and one way or another he might've incriminated himself. Some sort of stumble forward might've been made.

But there'd be no challenge because there was never going to be a chance to talk to him. Not at this rate. St. Paul's was the second con job on trusting Ramsden. The nearest I'd get was going to be in the crowd at the Albert Hall tonight. Before and after, at the Hilton, in his taxi, redcoats would ring him.

As for entering his Hilton suite . . . After his Tudor Inn lapse, after losing his attaché case, he probably had his Hilton suite booby-trapped.

The outlook was bleak as the temperature. I'd no way of knowing that my efforts were going to end so badly, but I remember thinking, frigid beside Dr. Johnson, that I ought to forget the whole wretched business, put the Reverend out of my mind for ever.

Here he came.

Alone, distant, but bearing down, purposefully advancing, looking up and around at monuments, piers, the barrel vaulting, ever the awed enthusiast, the former guide, storing ideas for his own Creation World at Little Rock, built from the cash of four murdered Arabs. His big moon face turned to left and right above the white opera scarf and sombre evangelist's overcoat with astrakhan collar. There was no dodging out of sight behind Samveli Iohnson because the block he stood on was against the ambulatory wall. Behind me was an empty, clammy chapel which had been roped off.

He'd probably already spotted me. Unless I made up my mind in the next five seconds, and fled, we were going to meet. After too long a-smouldering my nerve was on the point of leaving me—inexplicably, I almost said. But the explanation, weirdly, was his being alone. I'd expected the entourage, the bully boys. In a spooky way, on his own he was more intimidating.

He'd stop at Dr. Johnson's statue whether he'd noticed me or not. I walked towards him.

He didn't stop, though he slowed, generating a flowery reek of after shave, looking ahead towards the glass mosaics on the choir walls and vaulting.

"Why don't we do a tour?" he said, and strode on.

I fell into step at his side. He'd turned right and was heading towards the marble pulpit as though that for him were home, though he didn't stop when we reached it. I was on the side nearest the pulpit, and as we walked past I glimpsed, just beyond it, a tourist with a guidebook who was coloured. I performed what those of us who have trod the boards, even in an amateur capacity, describe as a double-take, because I thought I recognised the singer, Bobby Foster, the one I'd met in the restaurant. But he'd turned his back, and I couldn't have sworn it was he.

The Reverend hadn't noticed, he'd right-turned again, and was striding on. I caught myself glancing about for Pet Aversion, but I didn't see her.

"I don't know what you've got against us, Pete, but I'm asking you to give us a break, stay off our backs." Like some upper-class toffee-noses I've interviewed, he never looked at me when he spoke, he looked away at columns, and up at the dome, and everywhere except at insignificant

me. "You don't have to agree with everything we stand
for, of course you don't, though let me tell you that more
and more people do, and we reckon we're doing a fine
job. I'm not going to quote the scripture at you, either,
though I'm sure it'd help show you the way. I'm asking as
a favour, Pete, a personal favour to me and my church."

We'd passed under the dome, walked by the monument
to Nelson, and the stairs up to the library and galleries,
and were heading along the aisle back towards the entrance. Or in the Reverend's case, it occurred to me,
perhaps the exit. When he'd said we should do a tour, had
he meant tour, touristic and leisurely, or turn? One turn
round the nave, then out?

I said, "Can we sit down? I thought this was an
interview."

"Hope to see you at my press conference, Pete. You'll
be able to ask all the questions you like. Tomorrow,
eleven o'clock."

This was utter anticlimax. Bathetic, pathetic, meaningless.

He was walking briskly, as if whatever he wanted to say
he'd said. But what'd he said? Was it finished, the interview? I had to stride to keep up.

"Seven years ago you lost a tooth in Eastleigh." Too
many teeth filled my own mouth, judging from the unnatu-
ral sound of my voice. If Professor Higgins had heard me
he'd have identified more Manchester than National Theatre. "It was me lost your tooth for you. You drove off
with four Arabs. Now can we sit down?"

He kept walking. There was nowhere to sit, all the
chairs were behind us, the entrance—exit—just in front.

"Because my questions aren't about God," I said in
mounting desperation.

"I don't comprehend your asseverations, Pete."

"Don't you? The police will."

"Pete, do I have to spell it out? You have the wrong
man."

He pushed through the revolving glass door, out of St.
Paul's into drizzling rain, and started down the steps. I
scurried, keeping pace.

"I've got the right man—"

"There are places for people like you, Pete. Go see a doctor. You'll be taken good care of."

"It's you who'll be taken good care of!" I must've sounded shrill, all the long smoulder combusting into flame which didn't even singe him. "The Old Bailey's over there! Look! You'll be taken wonderful care of—for life!"

I hadn't been aware of the limousine which drew up at the kerb as we loped down the last steps, though I imagine it was all that concerned Jody James. A chauffeur in a tan uniform hurried round to the rear passenger door and opened it for the Reverend.

"Haven't you missed your attaché case by any chance?"

"Nice to have met you, Pete."

"You're going to miss your spare tooth? What when someone smashes the one you're wearing? Will you whistle for donations? Whistle your prayers? The police are going to match up your teeth! You're finished! Why won't you talk!"

During this outburst he'd entered halfway into the back of the limousine, but now he turned and looked at me. The same spooky blue eyes that had fixed me in Eastleigh. There the rain had been heavier, and he'd been the chauffeur, with cap and stubble beard. More than once I'd wondered if that beard hadn't been started as camouflage the moment he'd arranged to chauffeur the Arabs.

"Pete, you're ill. Like I said, stay off our backs. Or you're going to be iller. The Lord has ways and means."

He climbed in. The chauffeur shut the door and stepped round the front of the car.

His Pastorship, without giving me another glance, had sunk back in plushy upholstery. I think I took hold of the door handle, trying and failing to open the door. I may've run some distance with the limousine when it started off, holding the handle. I was in such a state I don't remember too well what I did.

What I did do, some thirty seconds later when daylight dawned, figuratively speaking, was go home fast.

Fast meant the underground, which wasn't invariably

reliable, but for that part of London, at that hour, probably
was the quickest transport available, unless you had a
bicycle, or were a marathon runner. I was certain I was
going to be too late.

Much of life seems to consist of the certainty there's
little hope, but of flogging on anyway because of the equal
certainty you could be wrong, being wrong about most
things most of the time. That's how I saw it, charging for
the tube, and feeling thoroughly depressed. Worse than
there being little hope was there being little hope and
doing nothing about it, then discovering there was something you might've done.

Why'd Jody James taken the initiative in giving me this
exclusive noninterview in St. Paul's? Or anywhere. The
venue was unimportant so long as it was a fair distance
from my flat. I'd played slap into his hands. I hadn't
interviewed him, he'd interviewed me. He'd given away
nothing while I'd told him who he was and, as good as,
what he was, and that I'd got his false tooth.

On the tube the conviction grew that the point of the
interview hadn't even been who was interviewing whom.
It'd simply been to get me clear of my flat. If the office
had told him I'd taken today off, he couldn't have been
sure I wouldn't be spending it at home, installed, every
minute of it. The interview, at last the exclusive, had been
the carrot to tempt me out.

I'm near the top of Rosslyn Hill, midway between
Belsize Park and Hampstead tube stations, the not too
oppressively pokey basement in a Victorian mansion converted into a warren. There's a pleasant wilderness of a
garden, sufficient substance in the walls to dampen the
late-night stereos, and an absentee landlord. He has to be
absent. With the rent he charges, if he showed himself
someone would garrotte him. By the time I was crossing
the zebra, watching the front of the house, I was far from
sure I ought to be hurrying. Shouldn't I be staying well
away at least until curtain-up tonight when they'd all be
flexing their smiles, not at my flat, but at the Albert Hall?

You hear conflicting opinions on what to do if face to
face with burglars. You keep a poker in the umbrella

stand, and a pepper shaker handy somewhere, and you swing into action with these, and a hatpin, and mace, whatever that is. I've read about mace. Whatever it is, it's illegal in Britain unless it's the stuff you sprinkle into fish stew, and that's where you sprinkle it. You're not supposed to sprinkle anything into anyone's eyes. Anyway, either a weapon of some sort, or you close your eyes and surrender. In fact, opinions don't differ all that much. The police, and they're the experts, recommend the latter. Discretion as the better part of valour. If there were going to be the least chance of a replay of the knee and fist I'd had from Chinless, I agreed with the police.

So after the dash from St. Paul's I was now slowing down across the zebra, cold and rained on, very irresolute, not eager for my flat to be broken into, but not passionate about walking into the knees and fists of born-again housebreakers either. As well I did slow, because there they were, three of them.

Perhaps I should've been flattered by the strength of the team. Their heads were visibly on the move beyond the untrimmed privet. If I'd sprinted I'd have blundered straight into them.

Unless they were tradesmen, or rival revivalists, they were probably Jody's boys. I could see only the short-haired tops of heads. They weren't Mormons because Mormons travel in pairs, or they have when they've visited me. Whoever the heads belonged to they'd come from my flat because it's the only one with its entrance round that side of the house. All the others are up the steps and through the front door. I'd have made for my car and watched from there, only it was at the garage, something to do with the brake fluid. By the time the heads had reached the gate I'd ducked out of sight behind one of the cars parked illegally, bumper to bumper, at the kerb.

The car I crouched behind was a Datsun, going by the word spelled out two inches in front of my eyes. I lifted my head, looked through the car's windows, and ducked down again. They were heading my way in their snug mohair, and not dawdling. The Datsun was theirs, obviously—what in the world was more to be expected?

From this second glimpse Chinless was not among them. The one carrying the red attaché case was the steward who flashed the gold molar when he smiled, which he wasn't doing now.

Crouching, a worried Datsun owner, I perused the tyre which had been causing so much trouble, tied shoelaces, sought the dropped contact lens, and out of Datsun got stun, stand, sand, ants, nuts, tuna, and unsad, while passers-by passed by through cold and wet, unconcerned. By now the trio must've passed by too, for there were no Datsun doors opening and closing. No voices, shadows, anything.

Cautiously, I straightened up and looked over the roof of the next car. Bundled up in their winter coats, the stewards were climbing into a car farther down the hill.

When the car started up the hill I waddled onto the pavement and squatted, out of sight, perusing tyres for punctures, as the stewards accelerated by. I watched them out of sight. I was furious at this invasion of my flat, and queasy too, because they'd outnumbered me, and it'd been what Wellington, I think it was Wellington, had called a damn close-run thing. I straightened up again, except I only half straightened up, because now entering through the gate, and turning left the way the redcoats had come, along the path to my flat, was somebody else I knew. Possibly I should've hailed him and introduced myself, but I didn't, and that's that. I was dumb. I froze in a stooped posture. Anyone who'd seen me would've guessed lumbago. If anyone did see, they didn't rush to help. They mind their own business in my part of London.

I bent down again to inspect the tyres, and listened to the very faint ringing of my doorbell. He was wasting his time. I decided I'd accidentally walk into him when he came out through the gate, because I was sick of mysteries, and sick of these armies of visitors. Then I decided I wouldn't. In the next fifteen minutes I changed my mind fifty times. Would, wouldn't. Would, wouldn't.

I say fifteen, which is what it seemed like. More than likely it was no more than four or five. And when I say I knew him, what I mean is I'd seen him before, in the corridor at the Tudor Inn, with his meat pie and dragging shoelace. The one who'd known me. I couldn't guess how he'd known me but he'd called out my name.

Five minutes or fifteen, I seethed while I waited, and the longer I waited the more furious and sick I became. He wasn't waiting, he'd gone into my flat. The bell had stopped ringing, and as you don't stand five minutes waiting for someone to answer a bell which you're not ringing anymore, and he hadn't reappeared, and there was nowhere else for him to go, he had to have gone in.

I'm not proud of this, but as I'm trying to be inclusive as well as honest I should add that I terrified myself wanting to pick up one of the round stones in the garden, and rush in and smash him with it. I wanted to, and I think it was a toss-up whether I might've done so or not. After Jody in St. Paul's, then the stewards in my flat, and now this individual, I'd had more than enough. There was that hot, vomiting, never-again sensation in the throat and eyes, the same as when for the first time you've seriously drunk too much, and all you want to do is die.

Low on my list of guesses was that he'd be the police. But I'd rejected my earlier guesses. He wasn't the press, as I didn't know him, and while there are plenty of press I don't know, this one just wasn't a reporter. I don't know how you could tell but you could. He wasn't a religious canvasser because, again, he simply didn't look it. He wasn't jaunty enough to be selling insurance, he wasn't carrying encyclopaedias, and though he might've been reading gas meters, he didn't carry a bag, or anything at all, and if he were from the Gas Board, what was he doing entering my flat?

He might've been the police after all. Conceivably they might've resurrected the Pithley affair and be seeking out the star witness, though doing so at the same time the Reverend had arrived in Britain was too much of a coincidence. If he were the police, one inquiry he'd not be mentioning in his report was the one he was making in my flat. I'm not a lawyer, but I'm sufficiently versed in the rights and liberties of Englishmen to know that unless he had a search warrant he was committing trespass as much

as anyone else would be, and magistrates don't sign search
warrants except as a last resort.

Bobbing along on the other side of the privet came the
man's hat, in the hatband a tuft of stuff like something off
a Christmas tree. I heard the gate close, then his tread
along the pavement on the other side of the car. The rain
was sluicing down, but he was singing to himself. What he
was singing, of all things, was that BAGS song about
counting on the Man at the Wheel. Fairly tunelessly, I
thought. From the snatch I heard before he was out of
earshot, tramping down the hill, he didn't have either the
words or the tune anywhere near correct.

The door into my flat had been forced. The wood was
splintered, the lock askew and coming away. Either the
stewards had been completely without expertise or they
just hadn't bothered.

If the door hadn't been damaged I doubt I'd have been
aware anyone had broken in. Apart, that's to say, from
having seen them leaving. But the place was not only
unsavaged, it was untouched by human hand, or looked
so. I'm reasonably tidy, I know where things are, and
everything appeared to be as it should. Except for the red
attaché case having gone from the bath.

All right, I knew it'd gone because I'd seen it go. In a
stage farce there might've been numerous identical cases,
but I was finding none of this farcical, and it never occurred to me that His Pastorship wasn't in the process of
having returned to him what was his. What I did find
curious was the impulse that drives you to where what's
gone has gone from, when you know it's gone, simply to
gawk at the empty space. Still, not to have checked, I
suppose, would've been odder.

So much of the past five days had been outside my
experience that I hardly knew anymore. The line between
what made sense and what was batty had become a thread.
I mean, the most recent example, I don't make a habit of
waddling round cars, hiding from Little Rock programme
sellers, and strangers with decorations in their hats.

And if keeping stolen goods in the bath sounds batty, I

should explain that the bath's in the kitchen—that's the kind of conversion these flats are—with a hinged lid which is useful for chopping onions on and eating off, when it's down, though you have to perch sideways. You might not even realise that here was the bath, so long as you ignored the taps at one end. Visitors haven't always realised this was the bath, not immediately.

As a hidey-hole the bath was still batty, but no more so than the wardrobe at the Coronet Suite, if that'd been intended as a hiding place. But if you've never tried, hiding an attaché case isn't the simplest thing in the world, and in my flat it was impossible. There were the cupboards, under the bed, or in the bath. It wouldn't surprise me if mine weren't the only pad where hiding an attaché case presented problems.

I had two present problems. One, unwinding. The fridge was bare of beer. On the shelf was scotch, crême de menthe for visiting courtesans, and a nasty French aperitif tasting of nettles and dust. I put the kettle on for tea.

Second problem. Either the insurance or the landlord ought to cope with a new lock and door, or portion of door. But they'd expect the Hampstead peelers to be told. The insurance would insist. I'd have liked the insurance to pay, not me. But I didn't want the peelers told.

"So what's missing, sir?"

"Ah yes, well, there was just this attaché case."

Priorities! Vexed about who'd pay for a new lock, while for all I knew the Reverend James was hatching my permanent exit out of his life!

The tea brewed. I mooched. The doorbell rang.

My nerves weren't what they had been. Listening to the bell repeat itself, I stood doing nothing about it in the middle of the sitting room: threadbare carpet, gas fire, comfy, overstuffed armchairs, a divan for the occasional overnight guest, too many books and records, and as *pièce de résistance* a cluttered mahogany table big enough to seat a dozen for supper, though it never has, not in my time. The bell was now silent.

There was no one I wanted to see. Gas-meter man, window cleaner, April, stewards, police, nobody. After a delay long enough for the visitor to have given up and be retreating along Rosslyn Hill, the bell started up again, and I went to the door. At least it wasn't going to be stewards, back to repair the damage.

On the other hand, it wasn't far off. Same genre.

"Well," I said, staring.

"Sorry." She stared too, though she'd known who was going to open the door. Perhaps it was my cuts and bruises. Abrasions and contusions, the Eastleigh hospital always called them when they gave you a patient's progress. Last time we met I'd been unmarked, a rosy cherub. "I had to have a word," she said, "but very quick, okay? I won't come in."

I hadn't asked her in. I didn't want her in. Her coppery frizz bedraggled, green eyes bright, overall air farouche and tense, she was an unsmiling Medusa not needing to come in because she could just as easily commit common assault from the doorstep. I glanced down at her hands for retaliatory Golden Syrup. Nothing. At her hip, hanging from a shoulder strap, was a buckled leather bag capacious enough to have held a carton of syrup tins.

"Come in," I said. "Just a step, if you insist. It's either you or the rain."

After a moment's indecision she stepped in. I shut the door, as far as it would shut. I had to thump it. Wood splintered, the whole lock assembly jolted farther askew.

"Fix it one day," I muttered. "Been like that for weeks."

"It's been like that ten minutes. Are you going to the rally tonight?"

"Are you inviting me?"

"Are you or aren't you?"

"It's my day off."

"Ah." She stood there nodding, the tension seeming to seep out of her. "You're not going."

"Might go as a customer. Sing along, y'know?"

"No, don't."

"Did your Reverend send you?"

"No one sent me. Look, we're not crazy about each

other. Like it could be the word is loathing. But just please stay away, tonight and evermore. Please?''

"Yes, Mummy. You don't want to see my legs broken?"

"I don't know what you're trying to do, I guess it's all for your newspaper, but I know them."

"What do you know?"

"Please." She reached for the door. "That's all."

"It's not even a beginning. Take your coat off. Tea's made."

"Sorry."

"If you tried me with a couple of explanations you could stop saying you're sorry all the time. You can't breeze in and tell Caesar not to go to the capitol just like that."

"What capitol?"

" 'Do not go forth today.' Calpurnia. 'You shall not stir out of your house today.' "

"Good-bye."

" 'Bye. See you tonight. Good luck with the arpeggios in the diatonic. Lots of *sforzandos*. Be rooting for you."

She did nothing for a while except face the door. Then she came into the room, very grudgingly, I thought. The look she gave me was a glare. Exasperation, resignation, detestation.

I lit the gas fire. In the kitchen I muddled about with spoons and milk, giving her time to concoct whatever story she was going to tell me. Or to leave if she chose.

Or relax. When I came in with the tray she was sitting unrelaxed on the edge of my favourite horsehair chair, parking her bag at her feet. Most women in her rained-on state, left alone, would've run a comb through their hair. Pet Aversion didn't look as though she owned a comb. Or would've known what to do with a hairpin.

The reason she kept to the edge of the chair may have been so as not to wet it with her coat, on which point she'd compromised, unbuttoning it but leaving it on.

"Milk? Sugar?"

"Sure. Anything. All I can tell you is most of our church they're straight, good people. Christians. But there's a handful. There has to be, because we meet these complete crazies, so what it comes to is self-defence. Okay, and there could be the Old Testament thing too. You know, an eye for an eye.''

"Or broken legs.''

"I tried to warn you. I'm still trying.''

"Why?''

"I'm squeamish. Isn't that soppy? I've read the New Testament.''

"You're the only one who has. No one else is warning me.''

"No one else knows you exist. I'm the one you gibbered to about our Pastor. Supper at the Tudor Inn, remember? What was it—crazy racist? Fingers in the till? Something about dead caliphs? You won't remember, you were stoned.''

"Thought it was your singer colleague I was gibbering to—Bobby Foster?''

"Plus our chief steward behind you waiting to get a word in.''

"Ah, him.'' After which I was enemy *numero uno*, meat for the handful who hadn't read the New Testament. I swallowed a mouthful of Darjeeling. "All the same, Mr. Foster didn't try to warn me.''

"He warned me. Said I'd be out on the street with my suitcase if I spoke to you, if I interfered. If it was found out I'd interfered.''

"But you went ahead. And you're still a BAGS singer, onstage tonight.''

"Bobby's warning wasn't a threat. It was advice. Oh, this is pointless.'' She reached down for her bag. "Are you genuinely so cynical, or is this your role as worldly newsman?''

"I was wondering about your role as the squeamish, sensitive handmaiden of God. You'd not by any chance be lending your steward comrades a hand?''

"Hand in what?''

"Come on, you know they were here. Ten minutes that door's been broken. You told me. How d'you know?''

"Saw them break it. Okay, heard them. I must've arrived about a minute after they did.''

"But naturally they didn't see you."

"If they had I'd not be here now."

"I know. You'd be on the street with your suitcase. Why couldn't you have phoned?"

"I tried. No answer. Anyway, I figured you might take more notice if we met. I was wrong, wasn't I?"

"No, you were probably right."

"Why were they here?"

"You tell me. You've told me nothing yet. Break a few legs?"

"So why didn't they wait?" She leaned forward from the edge of her chair, a conspirator needing to know. "Did they take anything?"

"What would they take?" I looked round for something they might take. "Let's be perfectly frank, as the politicians say. You betrayed me."

She might've been soppy and squeamish, frightened of what the stewards perhaps intended for me, and brimming with anxiety and advice. And she might not. At that time I'd no way of knowing. Her bony face was registering disbelief and injury.

She said, "How betray?"

"The Tudor Inn, when I phoned you for cocoa and gave you my room number, all you said was I'd got the wrong number. Five minutes later in came your redcoats." I switched on and off a smile to indicate the unappealing result. "I had the impression they thought they were protecting their own. With overkill. 'Vengeance is mine, I will repay,' sayeth the born-again heavies."

"I never answered that call. It was Roberta, my roommate."

"Is Roberta the steward with no chin?"

"Oh my, you're humourous. There were seven of us, including two stewards, which was your tough luck. We split into sevens each evening for Orisons. That's prayers and roll call. Another fifteen minutes they'd have been gone. You'd have got me."

"Or Roberta." No doubt Roberta had thought she was doing her born-again duty, announcing the cocoa call from the rooftops. "All right, sorry. Your tea's getting cold."

She hadn't touched it. Now she stood up, buttoning buttons, hoisting onto her shoulder the bag's strap.

"So you'll stay away tonight," she said.

" 'And for thy humour I shall stay at home,' " I said.

"Because truly, I know these jocks. If you keep nosing in, I promise you, the next sticky situation's going to be yours."

Her expression was expressionless, almost tremulously deadpan, her green eyes on mine, watching for the reaction. I obliged with matching deadpannery.

Under other circumstances I'd have brought out the crème de menthe. In spite of everything my impression was of splendid potential—fun, originality, warmth, horse sense, and it wouldn't have had to be imperative, given proper caution, to have grazed one's skin on her bones. She hadn't once tried to sell me the born-again line either. I should've at least walked her to a bus stop.

But the circumstances were as they were, the times were out of joint, and I needed to be alone. Whether Caesar would or wouldn't go hence tonight required thinking about.

I opened the broken door and let her out into the rain.

I walked up to the village for a curry, then went to the garage to see about my car, then shopped around for a carpenter who might be prepared to fix my door ere the summer, then settled into a catching-up session in the library. I was out of my flat most of the afternoon. When I returned, they too had returned, and gone again. I suspected that if I'd arrived back much earlier they'd have been waiting, but you don't hang on indefinitely when you've got the big spectacular looming, and you have to count the programmes and iron your jacket.

They'd done a thorough job. The place was comprehensively bulldozed, everything ripped and smashed, carpets torn up, chairs, mattresses, and cushions slashed, their stuffing strewn, and in the kitchen every pot and jar which might've hidden a false tooth upturned, the contents spilled out. I trod through glass and marmalade. The floor was like a transport café after the SAS had jaunted through.

Jody couldn't have listed for them, I reasoned, what ought to have been the contents of his attaché case. If he had, the hunt would've happened when they'd arrived the first time round, and found the case to be toothless. If he still preferred not to discuss his tooth, the search-and-destroy assault might even have been his own handiwork. Either way, he'd been out of luck. His spare tooth was in the keeping of Dr. Johnson, in a marble fold at the back of his toga, which surely wasn't dusted more than once or twice between royal weddings.

What really got me about Jody and his jocks—jocks was going to be my word for today—was their assumption that Peter Ramsden must be thick as a plasterer's thumb.

TEN

"We Love Jody," informed a T-shirt worn over a dozen sweaters. (*Chf. Insp. Peckover at this point placed his hand on my knee, not for the first time. For the first time I told him okay. My motives were curiosity and exasperation. I had no intention of permitting familiarity. The patient withdrew his hand instantly. P.O. Kremer.*)

In a doorway a group of girls and boys with guitars and a tambourine were singing about the Man at the Wheel.

They might've been waiting for a rock concert. Instant emotional satisfaction was the knack of the Jody James brand of evangelism, or for all I knew of every kind of evangelism. Gawd, the life of Riley! No dreary messing with endeavour, self-denial, theology, or tracking to the Orient to sit cross-legged, or to the banks of the Congo to swab the sores of lepers. Now I thought of it, they didn't give their ten per cent to famine relief. They didn't spend it on postage, like Miriam, firing off her Amnesty letters round the world. They gave it to Jody.

Watching the singers in their doorway was a constable with troubled eyes and a nose red from frostbite. I hoped it was frostbite, not alcohol, because he looked sixteen, and come the summer there'd be hope for an end to frostbite. He'd have been wondering whether he should do something about the doorway singers, whether an offence were being committed. Obstruction? Disturbing the Queen's peace? Nobody looked disturbed or obstructed, and the Albert Hall has thirty entrances, but all the same. I ambled on, sympathising. I remember the feeling. The last thing you dare do is seek out your sergeant for suggestions because you know he'll give you some.

Numbers-wise the crowd input situation wasn't up to the last night of the proms, but they were streaming in. Other T-shirts and lapel buttons told us, "God Made Darwin Too," which must've been the opposition—or perhaps not, I couldn't work that one out—and "BAGS—Not Fags," which was plain enough, and dispiriting.

Also dispiriting were the numbers of young people. Miriam had told me that suddenly in the States all these philosophy students—philosophy, for pity's sake—were sold on scientific creationism. No question, I'd have preferred not to have been here at all, unofficial God Squad or not, but Miriam had kept on about my duty to society, how I could file a report which might help keep the born-again lot out of the country if ever they wanted to return. Last time I'd been to the Albert Hall had been with Miriam. Free tickets from one of her archaeologists for Tchaikovsky's *1812 Overture* with live cannon and smoke.

At least it'd stopped raining. That left me feeling better about my uniformed colleagues who'd be languishing on the pavement until heads started getting broken inside.

Inside, I evaded the tables of knickknacks and records and headed for the stairs up, passing en route bearded Denis Fortune and his posse of gays, feminists, and lefties, all determinedly anonymous, but bulky, their furled banners and leaflets up their jumpers.

Seating procedure was first come first served. I didn't know where I wanted to be so long as I wasn't with the press again, or anywhere near the stage, where if there were going to be a Donnybrook, that'd be approximately where. The Albert Hall seats eight thousand, so there was space to breeze around, which is what I thought I'd do. Eight thousand Londoners wouldn't be leaving their TV sets on a November night for the Reverend Jody C. James.

First indication we didn't have a full house was the doormen—the blue, regular doormen, not the Reverend's redcoats—keeping people out of the stairways leading to the topmost tiers, presumably to save on sweeping up. The first two boxes I peered into were occupied, one with a

family eating sausage rolls, the next with a couple pouring
tea. The third was empty. I went in and looked down and
round.

Two tiers of boxes above me and the balcony and
gallery were empty. The crush below and in most of this
first tier of boxes I estimated at a couple of thousand.
About what you used to get on a Saturday night for a Gary
Cooper film when I was a nipper, when there were still
cinemas that were cinemas, not these coffin-sized conver-
sions huddled under one roof, and every chance of finding
your way into the wrong one. Gold and silver drapes,
massed flags, and the Great Awakening banner decked the
stage. The red-robed organist was already in action, squeez-
ing whinings out of his glittery electric box. The Albert
Hall organ was available, but it's got ten thousand pipes,
which may have been too many for him. Ideally, he'd
have been at one of those luminous jobs they had in the
Odeons and Gaumonts, the ones that went up and down
and changed from one ice-cream colour to another.

Stewards were patrolling, smiling, guiding. BBC and
ITN cameras were in place. I focussed on the press table
just below the stage, trying to pick out a bruised reporter
who might be Ramsden.

I didn't see him. Not if he'd been the bloke with the
attaché case in the corridor at the Tudor Inn. I wondered if
he'd had his interview with the Reverend James today, and
gouged a scoop out of it. For front-page revelations, see
tomorrow's *Post*.

I doubted it. That's to say, I doubted the revelations,
that there'd be any. I didn't know Ramsden, but I wasn't
enchanted by what I'd learned. Weak, ambitious, probably
a liar. Helen Goodenough hadn't been too adoring. He was
in hock to Desmond's, his fancy car was a mess, and
evidently you didn't make your fortune with a scoop. I'd
have bet fifty pence on him letting his newspaper stuff
itself while he went for a private transaction with the
Reverend, which was where the money was.

Right, wasn't my business to like him or loathe him.
But Mr. Foster had been nervous on his behalf. I'd have
bet another fifty pence on Mr. Foster being a copper.

Perhaps with that private lot—Pinkerton's, was it? The three "p's"—preacher, press, Pinkerton's. "Tooth and claw, sir . . . Ramsden's a dirty word . . . if everyone kept his distance, cultivated his garden . . ."

I was getting nervous myself. No one was keeping any distance at all. Everyone was growling and peeing like dogs in everyone else's garden. Preacher and press sniffing each other in an interview. Police nosing the bums of both. They were born-again stewards I'd almost walked into when I went to Ramsden's flat. They had the attaché case he'd been carrying in the Tudor Inn, or if it wasn't, it was bloody like it. If that'd been Ramsden. Press, police, preacher. Police, preacher, press. All permutations accepted and shuffled in the hat. Whatever else, they weren't keeping a distance.

Pamela, *cara mia*, underline this next bit in red, all right? If I'm on my way to the Grim Reaper, might as well go with a lily-white record, ho-ho, hark who's talking. It was not a question of breaking and entering, I only entered, the door being already broken.

Anyway, Ramsden wasn't there. No one was there. And they'd nicked an attaché case.

Where were we? Right, upstairs at the Albert Hall, and one or two at the press table below I believed I knew vaguely by sight, and one, a bespectacled young bean pole with an impressive forehead and a chin like Mr. Punch, I knew quite well. Richard Macdonald, *The Guardian*, sprawled forward over the table reading born-again literature which he held at arm's length. Was the arm's-length posture symbolic, or were there no lenses in his glasses? He'd probably heard there was a job at the Albert Hall and grabbed it, hoping for Verdi's *Requiem*.

Still, tomorrow I'd take a peek at *The Guardian*. There'd not be much about unedifying bloodletting at the Albert Hall, if that's what we were in for, but there might be half a page analysing creationism as myth and symbol in a democratic society, something to be brooded over by theologians and filed in university libraries.

Hall lights were dimming, stage lights brightening. Here they came. Scarlet files of gospel singers, angel-robed

soldiers of truth, God's task force, treading in march time
onto a shallow arc of a platform in front of gold and silver
drapes while the congregation applauded and whooped.
Mr. Foster was third from the left. He might've had the
beginnings of pneumonia and he might not. Impossible to
tell.

> "Born again!
> Born again!
> Fight for the right . . ."

I watched Mr. Foster gustily singing. Off centre sang
the bony redhead I was to hear about later, head thrown
back, jaws opening and closing like a claw on a building
site. At the time I'd no idea this was the one who'd tried to
warn us about Ramsden's legs, but she merited a second
look anyway.

I watched the press, sprawled and doodling, some talking, others passably attentive to the choir. Most of them—
not Macdonald, studying the handouts as if about to be
examined in them—from time to time looked round, regarding the congregation for signs of protest.

Far too early. The ITN cameras panned the choir, either
practising or already filming, determined on breasting the
tape ahead of the BBC. Red jackets speckled the aisle,
vigilant for heckling, steering latecomers to remote, unde-
sirable seats. The audience sang with verve as inhibitions
fell away. Denis Fortune and the couth London combatants
were a mute phalanx in a block of seats near a side exit.

Also in the audience, looking reasonably anonymous, I
spotted Reggie Hutchins, fanning himself with his hat,
and a colleague whose name I didn't know. Both Special
Branch.

The lighting had been showing off, fading and brightening, here dazzling, there crepuscular, and not pitchy everywhere except for the spotlight into which stepped the
Reverend James. The audience rose cheering. They were
some time giving their helmsman a chance, though he
could've got on with it if he'd really wanted.

"My friends. Dear, good friends . . ."

The Bible was held aloft, and a one-time junior senator for Wisconsin came to mind, though I hadn't been trying to be sceptical, and this one wasn't deliberately going to misquote the Bible. But with the Good Book held high like a fetish, like some kind of cabalistic totem which endowed its holder with omniscience and every supernatural advantage, no one was going to check up on what the witch doctor said it said, or challenge anything he said, any more than they had when McCarthy used to hold up his sheaves of papers and name names.

All right, some had. And some here tonight would be going to.

"The Gospel according to St. John, chapter three, verse three. 'Except a man be born again, he cannot see the kingdom of God.' My friends, shall we stand?"

Those who'd just sat down stood up again. My feet were perished. I left the box and walked with a stamping, warming-up tread. The curving corridor was as bleak and echoing as a prison. Occasional warders manned the stairways. I opened random doors into cells and saw prisoners at prayer. A mixed prison. Whole families, committed. On the opposite side of the corridor the alcoves which at a concert or boxing match would've become bars, come the interval, where barmaids already would've been lining up glasses, pouring preparatory tots, were deserted. I couldn't recall the Reverend's line on the demon drink. Odd if he didn't have one. He had one on everything else.

"Use a little wine for thy stomach's sake." Proverbs? Thessalonians?

Once on the farther side of the tier, for a different angle on the proceedings, I again started opening doors in search of a vacant cell. Some un-Christian looks from those in possession met me. I was on the point of giving up when I found one. Newly vacated, from the stink of it, by a clique of warders who'd been in there for a drag.

I think I nodded off. The singing was fine, but the Pastor was tedious, so far anyway, telling us about himself, how he'd come to be born again, what wonderful, sweet people we were, how wonderful London was, and our sweet, wonderful Queen, whom he'd be meeting on his next visit when his schedule wasn't so tight, and interpolating between these ramblings, and songs from the gospel singers, chatty prayers to God with the familiarity you'd usually keep for your neighbour, the bloke in the semi next door, who was a great geezer, four-square dependable if ever you were in a spot, though maybe a bit soft on communists, welfare scroungers . . .

Assuming he kept to his pattern, and the opposition to theirs, there'd be no scrummaging until after the passing of the plastic buckets, and the intermission.

The press looked drugged. Macdonald alone was in motion, though of such a minutely jerky, juddering kind, you'd have been unaware if you'd not watched closely. The top and back of his head and shoulders were towards me. I couldn't make out what he was up to. I think he was cutting his nails. I watched the audience again, seeking the Special Branch.

Then I saw Ramsden. The same bloke anyway from the corridor in the Tudor Inn. He wore a duffle coat and was sitting about halfway back in the middle of a row. Nowhere near the press table. I'd not have noticed him if he hadn't taken his hand from his face at the moment my gaze tracked in his direction. He banged his calf a couple of times, recrossed his legs, then returned his hand to his lowered face, contemplative. There wasn't a spare seat anywhere near him. His neighbour on his left was a black woman with a baby.

Onstage the Reverend was explaining "circularism"—how the Lord found ways of blessing with high wages and increased profits those who gave generously. "The comforts of wealth are just one way the Lord blesses those who put him first," he explained. The redcoats were in position with their buckets, ready for the off. I left my box and hunted along the corridor for the first stairs down.

Unless you're a regular the Albert Hall isn't too difficult to lose your way in. I didn't exactly get lost, but the door which ought to have given onto roughly the halfway point, near Ramsden's row, or so I judged, decanted me close to the stage. The aisle was jamming up with believers stretching their legs and patting their pockets for the contribution which unbelievably they might've left behind on the kitchen shelf. I dodged back into the corridor, now filling with refugees from the hall, and tried the next door along.

This was more it. I edged through redcoats and converts towards Ramsden's row. The black woman with the baby was using his empty seat as a table for thermos and oranges.

I watched the doors through which sinners and saved were filtering into the corridor. I looked along the rows immediately before and behind Ramsden's. He might've escaped for a smoke, if he were a smoker. Or to telephone the *Post*. I squeezed into the corridor and walked, searching faces, then doubled back.

I didn't see him. No matter. Presumably he'd be returning. Copy for the BAGS rallies came in the second half. Would he be returning to the same seat? Avoiding the press table, losing himself in the auditorium's crush, was reasonable if he was fearful for his legs. The corridor was fast becoming crowded with Christians.

"Mr. Peckover!"

I looked round. Macdonald.

He was bearing down beaming, delighted, jostled and jostling, Punchinello chin thrust forward, hand outstretched for shaking. I shook the hand.

He said, "Are you on duty? Good heavens! You've not been born again? You?" I wasn't sure I was flattered. "Have you?"

"Just curious."

"Splendid. We were going for a drink. Gracious, sorry— Dizzy, this is Henry Peckover, the poet, delicious occasional verses, some of them, you must know them. And Scotland Yard, of course. Isobel Wood—*The Times*. Do come. I mean, if you're not composing."

The nod *The Times* and I gave each other was mutually suspicious. Never mind she was a looker, probably with an Oxbridge degree in her purse, and when all's said, *The Times*. But that paper cuts no ice with me. All right, must be twelve years at least—the day the Yanks were up there walking on the moon—but it was *The Times* came up with the corruption among London coppers. End of an era. End

of a century of a tradition as the best sodding police force
in the world. The old respect gone for ever.

I sounded like some monocled Blimp. So a clean-up
was in order, and *The Times* got it right. All the same, you
can't expect me to be in love with it.

Macdonald was different. Anyone who thought of me as
a bard first, a copper second, was only tuppence in the
shilling, but he had my vote. Personally, I always thought
he was in the wrong business. His idea of news was an
anthropologist changing his mind over a Neanderthal occi-
put, or the third flautist with the Royal Philharmonic being
promoted to number two.

We had to scurry because in this neighbourhood the
nearest pub was a good four-minute scurry away. But a
coal fire blazed, the jukebox was stupendously silent, and
the beers arrived promptly. Macdonald wanted to talk
about the molecular structure of the hop. Something of that
sort. But he had to pause to swallow.

Casual as daisies, I nipped in with, "D'you know the
Post man—Ramsden, is it?"

"Who?" Macdonald said.

The girl said, "Peter Ramsden—why?"

"No reason." Bloody "why?" Who'd she think she
was talking to? "Saw a couple of stories he'd done on
these people, but no analysis. Just the demo. What I'd like
is debate, the background."

"You could be reading the wrong paper," the girl said.

You could be heading for a boot up the read end, I was
tempted to say, but settled for, "Is there any case at all for
this scientific creationism?" I was asking Macdonald.
"They're increasing, there's a load of them, they can't all
be charlatans, or stupid—"

"Why not?" interrupted the girl. "Since when were
numbers an argument for truth?"

"—and they've got plenty of big guns on their side, in
the States, school boards, lawyers," I said, riding over
her, hoping a hoof might catch her a glancing blow. "If
the science teacher gives ten minutes to evolution, he has
to give ten minutes—"

"You're talking politics, not theology," the girl said.

"—and in California—"

"God, California!"

"—a father sued a teacher for telling his son he'd evolved from apes." If I'd had a subscription to *The Times* I'd have torn it in small pieces and floated them in her bitter. "However you define fanatic, are they any more fanatical than, say, the College of Cardinals, or vegetarians, or Arsenal supporters? If you're going to believe in God why not go the whole hog and believe he started it all?"

"Yes, well, that's a cop-out. Ha!—no wordplay intended. Anyway, you're begging the question that God exists."

This time, to my relief, Macdonald, frowned into his beer. His attention hadn't seemed to be engaged, and the more the girl kept putting me down, the more I hoped he'd take over, put her down, and give me the definitive answer to the riddle of the universe. A couple of easy sentences which I could carry home to Miriam as my own.

"It's quite simply not reasonable that God exists, not in the sense of an all-knowing, loving, supreme being, because apart from anything else there's the existence of evil, though there's free will of course, and one might legitimately argue that reason's irrelevant anyway. So it's not entirely simple, though it's certainly demonstrable that God is the projection of purely human aspirations and fears. At the same time, he can be proved to exist by the traditional proofs, most of them perfectly adequate, such as First Cause, which holds up, I'd say. Also morally, because of conscience, and cosmologically—that's Aquinas, what a splendid man!—and teleologically, yes, predicating the necessity of an intelligent Planner, the alternative being mere trial and error, and ontologically, which was Anselm saying God's the highest conception we can manage, as humans, and since our highest humanly possible conception must exist, therefore God must exist. I'm not convinced that's not word-juggling. What would you say?"

"Well," I said. He wasn't seriously asking me, was he? "Tricky."

"I agree. Rather a mystic, Anselm, and a politician, kept getting banished then coaxed back. He deduced that if nothing greater than God could be thought of—see, I'm not happy with that for a start—and since existence would have to be an attribute of such a thought, then *ergo* God. Demolished by Kant, of course, another conjuror. Except that now philosophy is demolishing Kant and resurrecting Anselm. By modal logic. Of course, it's just as difficult to prove that God doesn't exist. Almost impossible not to believe in him, I'd have thought. I mean intellectually not to. Faith is something other, though that too may be subject to the laws of logic. It's really not my subject. What isn't in doubt, what's manifestly verifiable, though it's a sidetrack, is that for many—Christian, Muslim, Jew— God is where one returns when there's nowhere else. Like home. That's not terribly helpful either."

He fell silent. Whether celebrating or blank, there was no knowing. He looked troubled. After a fairly prolonged lapse of time he took off his spectacles, dipped one of the earpieces into his beer, stirred the beer, recovered the earpiece, and sucked it. He still said nothing. Perhaps he'd said it all. At least he'd silenced *The Times*.

"So you don't believe in God?" I ventured.

"What?" he said. A further pause. "No, no," he agreed, or disagreed, and after some time staring unbespectacled into space added, "I wonder if spiritual questing mightn't be something to be saved up for one's old age? A hobby to be held in reserve, like making patchwork quilts. If one reaches old age."

I don't think we touched on creationism, though I'd not have sworn to it. Macdonald was looking more troubled than ever. After another beer we trotted back to the Albert Hall, arriving almost too late.

The Reverend James stood stage centre with both arms raised.

". . . squash like a bug for his sake who suffered for us the sin which has no name . . ."

"Hey yes! Jody! Yea yea!"

". . . and render to us, Lord, the Cruise missiles we're going to need to contain the red communist hordes—"

"Pig Hitler! Back to your vomit!"

Denis Fortune. Whoever he was in fine voice, as resonant as the Reverend, though whatever else he had to say was lost in demonstrators' chorus, that mounting counterpoint of shouted abuse, responses from the vexed born-again community, and the Reverend James calling boomingly into his microphone for love. Banners had unfurled in two areas, evidence of both the independence and the agreed strategy of the north and south groups. A missile less lethal than a Cruise skimmed stageward with spectacular but not total accuracy, exploding on the lectern and streaking the Reverend's double-breasted self with tinselly yoke and albumen. He could've been hung on a Christmas tree, or simply hung—sorry, hanged—if the demonstrators had had their way. The redcoats converged.

Macdonald and *The Times* girl were moving fast and without a good-bye to the press table, to my mind a conditioned reflex, the press table being irrelevant. Any reporter with a nose for news—Ramsden possibly—would've stayed put, observing, or shunted closer to the banners, swung chairs, and fisticuffs, as I was doing.

Not too close. Not without the bonny boys in blue as reinforcements, and it was a bit early for that. First, they'd have to get their circulation going. Unstick themselves from the pavements.

"Good grief, it's Our 'Enry, thought you was with Immigration," said a voice.

Advancing past me was Reggie Hutchins, Special Branch, holding to his eye what looked like one of those old, black Russian Sobranie cigarette boxes. Perhaps they're around still, I wouldn't know. *Click*, went the box. *Click, click*. I kept pace. Someone barging past nudged the SB man and his box, resulting in a oath and a fuzzy snapshot of the roof of the Albert Hall.

"Have you seen," I said, "a bruised reporter, Ramsden, with the *Post*—oh, never mind."

He was advancing and clicking, not listening.

"Mate, Reggie, if one of these stewards comes at you and he's got no chin . . ."

Sod Reggie, onwardly clicking, a summer beach photographer who at any moment I expected to see handing out his card with astonishing cut-price rates. I looked beyond him towards the throb and tussle of the demo where redcoats and contributing Christians were engaged with the forces of darkness, and there was Ramsden.

He very nearly wasn't there, he'd only another yard to go, and in the next moment he was gone, dragged through an exit by three redcoats who had hold of his hair, arms, and one leg.

He wasn't the only one the stewards were ejecting, but to the best of my knowledge he was the only one whose legs had been threatened, and from the vigour with which he was being handled the threat looked as if it might be about to be carried out. I aimed for the same exit, Peckover to the rescue, jinking through the suburbs of the affray, then blocked by an all-comers wrestling contest which filled the aisle. I'd have preferred to have found a way round, but the packed congregation prevented that. To double back to the exit lower down would've lost time, and Ramsden, and I'd have lost myself hunting for him. As it turned out the dilemma was academic, as they say. Or *ergo*, as Macdonald might've said. Something hit me on the back of the neck. Down I went.

No idea what or who. Probably *The Times* girl. In fact it wasn't serious. It wasn't serious. It wasn't nice but it wasn't serious, not incapacitating, or not for more than a moment or two in the grand ocean swell of time.

When I was aware enough to find I was on the floor of the aisle, boots hopping over and into me, a carpet stink up my nose, this latest born-again barney seemed to be in progress much as before, a pandemonium of cries, thuds, grunts, and heaving bodies. In full voice through the loud-speakers carolled the gospel singers, either to calm us or urge us on. Something about flat racing and God the jockey, trampling the sinner, bringing home the winner. I looked up into a Sobranie box.

Click.

"This'll get you promotion, mate," Reggie Hutchins was saying. *Click.* "Or a dishonourable discharge. Either way, it's one for the files, too good to miss. Head up a little, please. Try not to smile. I'll let you have a colour print."

He'd gone, clickingly into a barrage, I hoped, or left and right hooks from stewards, or a demonstrator, one of the beefier feminists would do, I'd no preference. I rose to my feet and recovered my trodden hat. The heather had gone. I found the lower exit, the corridor, and the bluesuits streaming in, latecomers to the feast. But not Ramsden.

"Evening, sir." Sergeant Mattock tipping two fingers to his helmet, about to tell me he hadn't expected to see me here. "Didn't expect to see you—"

"Never mind me. Have you seen a young bloke in a duffle coat being hauled off by the stewards?"

"No, sir, can't say—"

"Get in there then. The rate's a quid for the goolies of anyone in a red jacket."

I wasn't going to find Ramsden, not in one piece anyway, but I went through the motions, turning up my collar and tramping, running, tramping again, round the Albert Hall, and into byways. Albert Court. Bremner Road. I looked in doorways, stopped to question the rare, remaining bobbies outside the Hall, and gazed into the concrete and brick spaces of Prince Consort Road for signs of life, or legs. I arrived back where I'd started.

There was now a fair amount of life, mainly the born-again squeamish who were choosing home in preference to punch-ups, and trickling from the Hall bearing their booklets and key-ring souvenirs. A copper approached along the pavement and told me that if I were still in the market, two of the red-coated stewards, though there may have been more, he'd not personally seen them, he'd been patrolling the south side at the time, they'd been sighted, these red jackets, running back to the Hall from the park.

"When?"

"Couple of minutes, sir."

"Where in the park?"

"Direction of the Memorial, sir. So I gather. One of the St. John's boys—"

"Come with me!"

The lights must've just changed because a surge of traffic along Kensington Gore kept us hanging about in the road's middle. I sprinted through the first gap, and with the constable after me ran across the pavement and towards the stone steps up to the Albert Memorial.

No one. The constable skirted round one side of the Memorial, I ran round the other. We met on the far side by a fence guarding trees and gardens. Though the more distant reaches of the park were in shadow, complete dark in places, here the trees and walks were lit by the road lamps and the lights of the Ring Road across the Serpentine. I ran on, but not far. On the grass beyond the angle of Lancaster Walk and the Flower Walk, under a chestnut tree, someone was crouching.

He'd heard our feet slapping the Memorial's surrounds because he turned his head and beckoned. A St. John's ambulance bloke, elderly and tubby, beckoning with what looked like a white hydrangea.

Cotton wool. In his other hand a bottle of antiseptic. At his feet lay his open bag of tricks, and Ramsden, stark naked.

"There's blankets and stretcher on the way," the ambulance man said, crouching, dabbing at wounds. He stood and started to take off his coat. "Bastards."

Ramsden's eyes were shut, his mouth slightly open. He lay propped on one elbow, chin and temple decorated with red flowers of cotton wool, his face uplifted as if for comfort and more antiseptic. The air reeked of the stuff. When he opened his eyes and saw me, or more probably the constable, and the St. John's uniform, he reached his arm up for assistance. His body was winter-white, but I reckoned it'd be blue if blankets or the ambulance man's coat didn't wrap him up quickly.

Hand stretched out, he began to struggle up.

"Stay where y'are, son," the ambulance man said. "Any moment now. You'll be all right."

Nobody took Ramsden's hand but he managed to stand anyway. He turned his back on us and started to run.

"Here!" the ambulance man said.

"Hi!" said the constable, and started after him.

"Wait!" I called to the constable, who stopped and looked at me.

Ramsden might've lost his clothes but he still had his legs, bicycling now through the grass, deeper into the gloom.

"Leave him," I said. "He'll not get far."

I believed he wouldn't. You don't flash through the middle of London, not even through empty Hyde Park on a November night, without the police wanting to join in. If the park's police didn't collar him he was still going to have problems getting a taxi to take him aboard. He might manage to nick a bike. But no matter what his means of locomotion, he'd never make it home to Hampstead.

I hoped he would. Or to his nearest mate's, or whatever refuge he might've had in mind. Perhaps he was hoping Desmond's Club might forgive and forget, or for all I knew he may have belonged to a more traditional club, the sort where they'd be too polite to notice when a member walked in bleeding and naked. He must've had a pretty strong reason for rejecting police assistance and a hospital bed. Why was he so desperate for his precious liberty?

A story for the *Post*—urgent, imminent—to do with the Reverend James and his church and yobbo stewards?

It'd have had to have been a meatier story, I'd have thought, than the Reverend simply hiving off a percentage from the plastic buckets for whisky and women. A story which visiting men of God, guests of the nation, thought it worth stripping and beating a homegrown reporter for.

Stripping him so he'd stay put, presumably. Which he hadn't done.

Or because they needed his clothes?

Whatever, letting Ramsden go seemed at the time the likeliest route to finding out. Perhaps we'd read about it in tomorrow's *Post*. As it happened, it'd have been kinder to have let the constable carry on and bring him down. But no one could've known that.

He was going well, Ramsden, a glimmer like a phos-
phorescent thread vanishing into the dark.

"There's his vest or pants, something, isn't it?" I was
pointing for the constable's benefit. Evidently they hadn't
wanted his clothes. Not his underwear anyway. "Start
searching. Careful how you tread.".

I tried to reach Ramsden from the Yard a couple of
hours later, which should've been long enough if he'd had
ways of getting home I hadn't thought about. Maybe he
had his Saab, bursting with new parts. His Hampstead
number went *brr-brr . . . brr-brr . . .* I got Division to
send a car, but he wasn't at his flat. He never went home.

Next day's *Post* carried tepid paragraphs on the Albert
Hall rally. No Peter Ramsden by-line.

Ramsden's vest, pants, shirt, and socks had been found,
but no shoes, suit, sports jacket, or whatever he'd had on
under his duffle coat. No duffle coat.

So perhaps they had wanted his clothes. Some of them.

No record of his having been admitted to any hospital.
No one picked up for trying to resurrect the streaking
mania. Who was Ramsden anyway, Division wanted to
know, and what was going on?

What was going on, without a please or a thank you,
was that my Bahawalpurans were misbehaving. Overnight
they'd transmogrified from cowed victims into indignant
subjects of Her Majesty demanding justice. Some lefty
organisation had passed them a copy of the nationality
laws. They were very excited, though I don't think they
could read. They fanned the document in my face and
gabbled accusations. The self-appointed leader, a creep
with a skinny moustache and no arse, kept demanding to
telephone Mrs. Gandhi.

That confused the issue, expanded it to madhouse dimensions, because I'd been under the impression Bahawalpur
was part of Pakistan. Was he a friend of Mrs. Gandhi
who'd crossed the border? The temptation was to hoist two
fingers at the lot of them and slam the door.

I'd nowhere near sorted it out when they, my Bahawalpurans, broke for lunch. I phoned the *Post*. After being

passed from department to department, I learned from the teaboy, or it might've been the managing editor, that Helen Goodenough was unavailable, Peter Ramsden hadn't been in and might be taking the day off, and the BAGS press conference had been cancelled. Compassionate reasons, illness of a relative in Little Rock, according to the Press Association's round robin, which the teaboy, or managing editor, had seen but didn't think he'd be able to put his hands on.

They'd left that morning, the teaboy said. Delta to Atlanta. Possibly Atlanta to Delta. Then Boondocks Airways, the one with the turnip greens and square dancing. My informant was a real cabaret turn.

I phoned Miriam. Sam had eaten half a bar of soap. Palmolive. Supper for the rest of us was the archaelogists' leftover baked bass.

Silly coincidence that, looking back. I didn't know it until the tourist literature came my way, but Arkansas was bass country. All Arkansans fished for bass. They had fibre-glass bass boats with depth finders and competed in bass tournaments wearing crash helmets and goggles.

At half past eight on my way home, I detoured to the Mucky Duck. Madam sat besabled on her bar stool like a weathered, wooden deity out of the British Museum's anthropology section.

"Peter still on his hols?" I asked.

"He's on a story," she said, and signalled to the barmaid.

"In Little Rock?"

"He'll hardly have arrived yet, dear." Smoke jetted at a tangent. "If you insist, I'll tell you the little I know, but I'd much rather you waited and bought the *Post*. Always assuming there's a story. We need all the new readers we can get."

ELEVEN

Little Rock had never been the sort of arena I'd have anticipated for my first big foreign story, any more than the most true and sorrie historie of the criminous preacher Jody C. James would've been my guess for the kind of book which'd be my first to reach the bookshops.

The Man at the Wheel. By Peter Ramsden. Not bad that, as long as people didn't think it was going to be about motor racing.

I can't see it won't reach the bookshops, unless the lawyers for the creationists find a way of stopping it. It's going to write itself. It almost has done, there being not a great deal more to say, apart from the mayhem.

Anyway, it was late afternoon with the light fading, and there I was in this hire car—rented car I think they say here—on leafy Adams Avenue, not a possum's hide's throw from Petal Merchant's house. Her parent's house presumably. There'd been only the one Merchant in the phone book. I'd been here two hours already and though it wasn't brutally cold it wasn't high summer. I'd turn the heater on, then off. Same with the radio. For retreads I had to head immediately for the Dan Curtis Tyre Mart on Sixth and Elm, but for peanut brittle and thirty cents off T-bone I was to hurtle to Kirschner's on Vine.

We had a twangy blue-grass number about Mommy's size-six wedding shoes, the ones she wore to bring the news. Then we had the temperature again. Thirty-seven Fahrenheit.

I ought to have felt exhilarated. But I wasn't a tourist, I

was in pretty horrible shape, and I couldn't have been more without a sense of holiday. I felt partly like a foreign correspondent on the trail, and partly like a Hollywood secret agent, as in the Tudor Inn foyer long ago, watching the BAGS gang strut past.

On my lap lay an Esso map of Arkansas from the glove compartment. I wasn't about to tour Arkansas, far as I knew, but the map was the right size for hoicking up in front of my face should she appear. Not that she'd have recognized me. I doubt my mum would've recognised me after the hammering the steward bastards gave me last night.

Correction, two nights ago. Was it? Dammit, was today Friday or Saturday?

Saturday. First of December. There was a great deal of Christmas about. Far more than in London. Downtown— that's the shops and theatres area—you could hardly move for Father Christmases ringing their bells.

Now they're ringing their bells, but soon they'll be wringing their hands—for Jody, favourite son, white hope, man of God, brightest star in the Arkansas firmament, misbegotten Messiah, murderer. Alas, poor Jody.

I might've felt none too perky, but I had resolution, and a sense of being close to the end of the trail.

I eyed the map. Little Rock wasn't New York or San Francisco, yet it could've been worse. Little Rock was at least the state capital, over a hundred thousand population, half of them Father Christmases. Agreed, you could've dropped several Little Rocks into Manchester and lost them, and big wasn't necessarily beautiful, but what if Jody's carpenter's shop and church and Creation World had been in any of these hopeless places outside Little Rock? Pine Bluff, Blytheville, Magnolia, Fox, Hope, they were all predictably homespun. But what about sexy Smackover? What about Blue Ball, Back Gate, Bal Knob, and Greasy Corner?

There was a Hamburg, and a Stuttgart. The Germans had arrived ahead of me.

The door to Petal's house remained steadfastly shut. On the roof was a fake chimney with a plywood Santa disappearing down it, or emerging. One or two lawns sported painted Santas and reindeer, and almost all had a Christmas tree. Helen would've screamed. She won't allow the *Post* to carry any reference to Christmas before about December the nineteenth, and froths if they creep into the paper regardless, as they do. A girl-child sagged along the pavement carrying a sack like Santa's and dipping into it, and tossing a rolled newspaper onto the lawn in front of each house.

Helen had agreed, a little grudgingly, to my mind, to my following Jody here. But she'd thought it worth a go. I'm not denigrating her, no doubt she was an effective journalist in her day, but it must be a while since she accomplished anything spectacular, and a Jody scoop for Christmas was what she hoped for. My guess is that her job isn't all that secure, and she knows it.

With the map came a leaflet. The Arkansas song was "Arkansas". Bird, mockingbird. First in bauxite, rice, and broiler chickens. Lowest expenditure per pupil of any state's school system. Good heavens, were they boasting?

Freshwater fishing, duck hunting, hot springs, eighteen million acres of forest . . . birthplace of Douglas MacArthur, Opie Read, Archibald Yell . . .

General MacArthur I knew about, but who was Opie Read? Who Archibald Yell?

No mention of Jody C. James. They were saving him up for a new category. Famous Arkansas Assassins.

Round the side of the Merchants' house came a boy bundled up in an anorak and woolly helmet, wheeling a bicycle. He leaped astride the bicycle as if it were Trigger and pedalled off down Adams Avenue. Petal's brother?

What would parents who called a daughter Petal call a son? Stalky? Leif, if there were Norse blood.

His exit left one fewer in the house. One fewer than how many? Was Petal there anyway? If I could've been sure of getting her alone I'd have pressed the bell, but I saw no future in her parents answering, and gossiping about a mashed-up limey who came calling on their daughter. They were probably bosom chums of the Reverend.

But I wanted Petal. Wanted her every way, naturally, but primarily to talk business, because I hadn't come this distance on *Post* money just to invite her into bed. She could enlighten me about the Reverend as boss, spiritual leader, psychopath, how he held his knife and fork, all the human touches that flesh out a story and which our readers lap up. Not least, she could give me an idea about his immediate schedule. My goal remained the heart-to-heart with Jody.

Once he knew I was there he might unleash his redcoats again, but I doubted it. I had that tooth. He knew I had it. Except he couldn't have been certain it wasn't now with the *Post,* or lawyers, or the police, awaiting my lifted finger.

Or—I faced it—awaiting my untimely end. My guess was that out of frustration, if not fury, and finally self-preservation, the Reverend was capable of trying to engineer my untimely end.

Problems after that, such as a tooth, he'd cope with when and if they arose.

I didn't see her come out of the house because I was twiddling the radio in a hunt for more of the blue-grass twanging. The first I saw she was in the drive hiking up the garage door.

She wore the same coat she'd unbuttoned but not removed in my Hampstead flat, and a woolly cap not unlike her brother Leif's, from under which spiked the ends of her copper frizz. I hoisted my map. If she saw me, son of Dracula with two black eyes and lips like a hamburger bun, she'd yelp.

I mentioned I wasn't in too great shape. There'd been a mauling from three stewards—Chinless as star performer— behind the Albert Memorial, and I was not at my prettiest. There was jet lag too. On top of which I was shivering still from my Athenian athlete's sprint through Hyde Park and much of Bayswater.

Achilles Ramsdenes, the Greek Streak. The Rump of the Short-Distance Runner. All I wasn't suffering from in that car on bosky Adams Avenue was triple pneumonia, and that could be only a matter of time.

For the Great Awakening finale at the Albert Hall I'd cunningly secreted myself in the audience, though what I was secreting was sweat, because five minutes after sitting down I saw Chinless watching me from the aisle. So at half-time I'd taken evading action and found another seat. But their eyes were on me. Came the demo, they'd plucked me up more or less bodily.

After the mauling, before the St. John's ambulance characters came trundling up, before I'd found breath enough to stir, all I could think of was that my car was on the road again. I'd collected it, driven to the rally in it, and it was at the Albert Hall waiting for me. No thought could've been more futile. The keys were in my jacket pocket, and the jacket and everything were gone. Presumably for scissoring up in search of the tooth they'd not found at my flat.

For the book I shall expand that dash, naturally, but at the risk of sounding like "With a bound Jack was free," I've nothing much to say about it now except it was a straightforward dash, the naked newborn babe striding the blast. And among my more horrendous experiences.

Physically horrendous, that's to say. Mental agonies drag on, but the dash lasted only seven or eight minutes from starting block to finishing post. Thanks to the proximity of an old flame.

Dashing, my thoughts had switched from my forlorn car to three other matters.

One, whether she'd be at home.

Two, keeping my bearings so I'd not dash in through the door of the Hyde Park police station just east of the Ring Road.

Three, my error in not having hung on another moment and borrowed the ambulance man's coat when he'd got it off.

Still, he'd been a Methuselah, he was taking for ever getting it off, and if ever he did get it off he might not've been a snip at letting it go. Some of these oldies have grips of steel, the result of constantly gripping your arm while they tell you about when beer was a penny a pint.

Spontaneity was what worked for me, bolting without a thought or a thank-you, though I was surprised the policemen didn't chase or throw things. The one in the hat was the one who'd snooped round my flat, who'd called my name in the Tudor Inn. He must've been keeping tabs on the BAGS tour.

I met no one in the park, though I recall at one stage a car honkingly in pursuit. Across the Bayswater Road and along Westbourne Terrace I met a few odds and sods, but not in the sense of stopping for introductions. The number of the house I couldn't remember, but I'd been to a party there once, and there'd been a boat at the bottom of the basement steps.

A boat was there. So, answering the door, was Marje, with whom I'd stayed fairly pointlessly in touch over the years. A nice irony, the door I pummelled being hers. But for Marje and her papa with his silkworms and newspaper I'd not have been ringing and pummelling anywhere, a refugee from stewards, because I'd never have seen Eastleigh or met the Reverend James in his chauffeuring period. I'd not have been here now, west of the Mississippi, on Adams Avenue.

These days she's a high-powered biologist at the London School of Tropical Medicine. She's not Marjorie Heap anymore. I don't remember her married name, but there are children, and her man's a boxing promoter, of all things, with a striped shirt and cuff links. She's slimmed down, but the hilarity's still there, and if she goes with hubby to his boxing matches I imagine she spends the evening falling about in stitches. When she opened the door she'd have laughed to bursting if she'd recognised me straightaway. Peter the playwriter from dear old university days, hands over his shrivelled, shivering frankfurter sausage.

But there was too much blood and cotton wool, so she couldn't, and she didn't.

Pet Averison wasn't going to crease herself either, but she too would be startled. If I caught up with her.

Before I'd folded the map away she was backing a spinach-green hearse out of the garage, then driving off down the road. I switched on and jolted off in pursuit.

Strictly, Petal's vehicle wasn't a hearse. But it wasn't a midget foreign job. Americans talk about the energy crisis but all they do about it is try and keep the Japanese cars out. The behemoth tooling along ahead of me would've been the run-of-the-mill family Ford or whatever—they all look alike to me—with dimensions such that I didn't see how I could lose it. My anxiety was in case I had to brake suddenly, or even gradually. I consider myself a more than competent motorist, but the car I'd hired had power brakes, which may be *vieux jeu* to Americans, but hadn't actually cropped up on any of my roadsters. No matter how soothingly I braked, the merest kiss of foot on pedal, the car would stop so violently I'd nearly be thrown through the windscreen—seat belt, seat, and all.

Five minutes and we were downtown. Santas, shoppers, excess traffic, and Jingle Bells janglingly jingling at one intersection, Little Donkey simpering at the next. I'd like to be able to say I was getting the hang of the brakes, but it wasn't so. Petal parked with stunning individualism and no warning. There being no slot behind her, I double-parked farther on, bracing myself as my foot caressed the brake, and halting with a squeal of tyres which would've enchanted Dan Curtis, bringing him to the door of his Tyre Mart with a beefy smile and his arms filled with tyres. When she crossed the road into the bank, a skinny singer in a woolly cap, listing from the bag on the shoulder strap, and curdling my loins when I ought to have been concentrating on business, and the headlines to come—after all that, I panicked onward and into a space a block away.

I jaywalked after her. Saturday evening at home you'd not find a bank open, but that's the difference between our two countries, unless here they were making an exception to net the Christmas spenders. Anyway, I'd thought she'd gone into a bank, but it was a Grand Ole Opry concert, Arkansas-style. Mountain music sawed and plucked from a lobby as shiny as an airport lounge. Looking in, I observed a hoedown with fiddlers and hand-clapping customers.

But it was a bank too, a poster revealed. First National City Bank—Ozark Crafts of Christmas. I was waiting for her on the pavement when she came out carrying a red attaché case.

"Hi," I said.

"Well, hi," she said.

Appropriately laconic, I thought, for this spot on the map. Who knew? Here, Billy the Kid and Calamity Jane may have played knucklebones together.

All the same, her eyes betrayed uncertainty as she stood stooped under the weight of case and shoulder bag.

"What've you got there?" I inquired. Though the case looked familiar, for all I knew they were BAGS issue, singers-and stewards-for-the-use-of. "Born-again key rings?"

"A thousand dollars, I think, I haven't counted it. It's for you from Pastor James. He said you're going to give me a small packet for him, is that right?"

"I don't have it with me. Can we go to my hotel?"

"Sure," she said, too quickly.

Everything about the encounter was wrong. But the stirring in me was the old Adam, and even if I'd not been jet-lagged, sandbagged, and generally comatose, I doubt I'd have tried to reason my way out of the possibilities ahead, uncertain as they were. From the moment I'd seen her onstage at the Princess Hall, a red-robed, copper-frizzed stilt, trilling her born-again hosannas, she'd been my kind of soprano.

If she were Jody's courier too, bringing unexpected loot, so much the better. How'd she known I was available for bringing loot to was a detail which could be gone into later.

Telepathic, she said, "I saw you from the house."

"So you phoned the Reverend?"

"Yes."

"Once upon a time you were trying to warn me against him. 'Take Ramsden off the story or they'll break his legs.' "

"They. Our stewards. Not the Pastor. He's a man of peace. They did that, didn't they—your face?"

That they might be contemplating doing it all over again was hardly believable. I'd have been readier to believe it if I'd been alert enough to look around and spot the mohair which must've been lurking. But I was too busy fantasizing about Pet Aversion, in my hotel room, in my arms.

". . . things fall apart . . . conviction . . . passionate intensity . . ."

"Yes," she said.

"Yeats," I explained, deranged. *"The Second Coming."*

We'd got on to religion, or I had. Fundamentalism and inerrancy. There's this conservative shift in religion worldwide, not solely in the States. Religion may be the opiate of the people, but as an intellectual I was naturally not incurious. Judaism, it's happening there, this getting back to the letter, the land, first principles. The Ayatollahs, of course. If she were an inerrant, fundamental believer, on paper anyway—between the sheets she was remarkably errant—she should've had some answers, if only those she'd heard in sermons from Jody. We lay entangled in my sanitized, chromed, veneered room at the Arkansas Traveller in downtown Little Rock.

"You've lost me, we've had the second coming, or I have," she said. "Aren't we on to the third?"

"Keep your eyes shut. Honestly, sorry about my face. You could turn off the light."

"I knew you were going to be vain. Stop talking about your face."

"What do they call girls from Little Rock? Little Rockers?"

"Little Rockets. It's because we're explosive."

Her coppery hair coloured the pillow like a painting of an explosion. I said, "This packet I'm to give you. The Reverend told you what it was?"

"Nope."

"You didn't ask?"

"You don't ask the Pastor. You listen."

She evidently listened to his suggestion, or order, for the greater glory of the First Born-Again Church of God, that she charm me. Where stewards hadn't succeeded, a singer might. It was plain as day. If he'd chosen her because she was the one I'd shown an interest in, the one I'd wanted to share cocoa with at the Tudor Inn, his choice was spot-on.

Sex plus cash. With one tooth all that was asked in return. A resistible deal to some, but not to me, or so, I surmised, Jody had reasoned. Willing or unwilling, Petal as bait. Was she naïve, sorry for me, or hypnotised by Jody the pander?

Whatever, she wasn't inquisitive about this mythical packet, and she didn't seem to want to talk about her Pastor. Frankly, she was interested in us. She told me that tomorrow, Sunday, I must be there, at the Homecoming Awakening Rally, where she'd sing like a bird only for me. She'd get me a ticket, it was tickets only. At two days' notice, the rally was going to be televised through seventeen states. The network had postponed Baptists from St. Louis or somewhere. I said I'd be there, which was the fib of the week. Anywhere the redcoats were, there would I no longer be.

When she went into the bathroom and closed the door I opened the red attaché case and counted a quarter of a million dollars.

That's a guess. Still, who's haggling over a thousand or two? There were twenty-five thoroughly ordinary brown envelopes, and the first two I opened contained each, in packets of ten, a hundred hundred-dollar notes. I looked in random envelopes from the bottom of the case and they too held hundred-dollar notes, each bundle of the same wedginess.

When she came out of the bathroom we played for a while. To have told her the case held rather more cash than she'd supposed might've confused her. Singers should sing. Worrying about the zeros was man's work. I went into the bathroom and was brushing my teeth when I thought I heard the door from the passage open, and voices.

I've said I was jet-lagged, and not thinking brilliantly. Instead of locking myself in the bathroom, I stepped back into the room. Not, as I was shortly to discover, that a locked bathroom door would have stopped them.

Chinless in his mohair stood in the middle of the room, hands in the patch pockets. He'd brought three others. The steward closing the door was the one whose gold molar gleamed when he smiled, which I expected him to be doing any moment now. Petal was wrapping herself in the bedcover.

I'd have felt sorry for her if I'd not been occupied worrying about my own prospects. Though she was here at the Reverend's command, her BAGS singing career was presumably ended. He was hardly going to be able to reinstate her after four stewards had seen what they'd seen, surprised her *in flagrante delicto,* or near enough. Bag and baggage, she was as good as out on the street.

"Believe I told you, sir," Chinless told me, "about insulting our womenfolk."

I believed he had. The situation was approximately the same, but a couple of variations were, one, that in my room at the Tudor Inn I'd been alone, I'd been insulting nobody, and two, on that occasion I'd had some clothes on.

It's bad luck being starkers because right away you're at a disadvantage. I'm the expert. I was making a habit of it. Having nothing to say, I said nothing, but headed for my clothes, which I'd draped over the back of the armchair by the TV. One of the stewards, not Chinless, or Gold Molar, but a chunky gofer with a shorn pate, arrived at the chair first, pulled the clothes onto the seat, and sat down on them, grinning.

Nothing further to be achieved from that quarter.

"So happens," I told Chinless, trying as best I was able to keep the wobble out of my voice, "you're interrupting a business transaction close to the heart of Mr. James. Before you make charlies of yourselves, you could check with him. Phone's by the bed."

"We're familiar with the business transaction, sir." At last, the smile. "Pastor James would be grateful for the packet, please."

"Packet?"

"Please."

Even if my wits have been flower-fresh I'd not have

known how to slide out of this. Tell them, which was true, I didn't have any packet? Tell they if they were talking about a tooth I still didn't have it, Dr. Johnson had it? Or tell them I'd left it outside in the car, if they'd just relax and amuse themselves while I dressed and slipped out for it?

Or that coppers were coming? Or I'd got a dodgy heart so they'd better not be rough.

Petal, it occurred to me, had known these smiling faces would be arriving. Once she'd charmed the tooth out of me, wrung my withers with dalliance and greenbacks, in they'd move to recover money and tooth, both.

I didn't believe it. You don't make love as she'd made love, all the sweet, steamy while waiting for the storm troopers to goosestep in and start bouncing your lover against the wall. She stood in her bedcover against the wall beyond the bed, her face turned to the wall. The red attaché case being a pace to my left, flat on the floor where I'd left it, its handle handily towards me, I took a pace to my left.

The fourth steward was a cropped blondie who ought to have been up in the mountains helping Mom and Pop with the chickens, but currently was a mohair ape, guarding the door into the passage. The shorn, chunky one sat grinning on my clothes. Gold Molar was turning on the telly. Chinless was telling Petal to go into the bathroom and get her clothes on, honey.

I grabbed the case, rushed into the bathroom, and slammed and locked the door.

The bathroom had no other way out—or in. Not even a window. I didn't need one. You hear about Yankee enterprise, ingenuity, get-up-and-go, the pioneer spirit, all that. What about Manchester enterprise? "Easy," as they chant on the terraces after the third United goal. "Eeeas-y."

I crashed my fist against the door for attention and bawled, "Quarter of a million down the bog if you don't clear out! Your Jody-boy's quarter million! Yours, BAGS money, flushed into wonderland—"

With a bang and a flurry of splinters, hinges, and mohair, the gimcrack door smashed in on me. The first one to arrive, slaloming along the door, was Chunky with a veneered splinter in the shoulder of his mohair, but I'd the fleetingest impression that all four were there. I was against the bath, supine and crumpled beneath half a door and Chunky with probably my back broken. No chance to dwell on the possibility because the door was kicked aside and hands were on me, dragging and throwing. I was relieved of the case, which improbably I still clung to. They seemed to be gassing and grousing a good deal, the stewards. Accusing each other of criminal negligence, I wouldn't wonder. One of them hit me on the side of the head. I supposed they'd had enough.

I had too. I might've been out, sleepy-bye, for a minute or two, or longer, or not at all. I recall looking up from the carpet and seeing Chinless in front of me on his knees opening the attaché case for all the world as if I might've found time to flush away two hundred and fifty thousand dollars. His mouth twitched. If he'd had a chin it'd have been ticking from side to side, saliva slobbering down. From the case he plucked a bottle of maple syrup which I didn't remember having been there.

At that point I didn't know it was maple syrup. The bottle was just a bottle, as opposed to a brown envelope. A squat, full, lightish-coloured bottle which smashed when it hit the wall, spraying the wallpaper with syrup. Chinless upturned the case, releasing a cascade of identical bottles, and not one brown envelope. I believed she'd have preferred Golden Syrup, because a girl like Petal would've had a sense of the apt, but probably you couldn't buy it here. Chinless was in a fine state, lips twitching, eyes goggling.

"Get after her!" he told someone.

I lifted my head, trying to take in what else went on in my Arkansas Traveller room. Not a great deal. One of the stewards was leaving, getting after her.

She'd gone. Her clothes too from the square of bedside rug where she'd let them fall. And her shoulder bag.

And a quarter of a million dollars.

Cleaning my teeth, the rinsing, spitting, meditating—how long had that taken? As long as she'd needed.

Chinless took off the mohair overcoat, then his jacket, holding out each at arm's length for collection by Chunky. Gold Molar turned the volume on the TV up high. A sit-com, judging from the fast talk and canned laughter.

While I'm confident I have several qualities well above the average, I was not sure I was worth all this. So little was left of me, fortunately, that I no longer cared.

TWELVE

"Here we come a-wassailing," carolled the Bard of the Yard, filled with breakfast, heeling-and-toeing back along Main Street.

Or Elm or Lincoln. I've been in the States before, don't think I haven't. No stay-at-home I. Every street's Main, Elm, or Lincoln, if it isn't First, Second, Third . . .

You count. Intoxicated, I was, on frosty abroad. I'd got other things to do than count.

Like breathing the Arkansas morning. Cough-cough. Frosty but clear. In the air a twang and a tang, a perfume of bare feet borne in on the west wind from the hills where the Johnsons were afeudin' again with the Jacksons. The sun was surely going to shine today on Our 'Enry, Immigration, God Squad, and, at five minutes' notice, Stateside, while the denizens of the Factory grumbled their envy.

Grumble away, old cockers.

My brief was to contact the city police with greetings and credentials. Then to liaise on coaxing one Peter Ramsden, hack, back to where he could write about the Christmas lights in Regent Street, preserve his legs intact, and be kept from dribbling grit into the reasonably oiled machinery of Anglo-American relations. Nothing to it. The sharp end of Ramsden's Fineliner pen was poised, if the assistant commissioner were to be believed, against the jugular of the Reverend Jody C. James, which might've been permissible, just, when the Reverend had been in

London, but could cause ructions now he was back on his home ground.

The AC expected me to swallow that?

I could believe there might be ructions. I could more easily believe that for reasons unbeknownst our newshound was bent on sticking his head above the parapet, and my AC and the police commissioner here in Little Rock were agreed it'd be simpler all round if he could be bundled home fast.

"Love and joy come to you . . ."

Half past nine, Sunday morning, and never have breakfast at your hotel is my motto. Not when you'd arrived only an hour ago and all there'd been time for was checking in and dumping your bag. Get out and about, see the locals, that's the form.

The only breakfast place open within five blocks had been a drugstore. Ha!—that term, "drugstore." Redolent exclusively of the U.S.A. After study of a door-sized menu lasting all of three seconds, I'd elbowed the hominy grits, hash browns, gumbo stew, blueberry griddle cakes, all such regional delicacies, and summoned eggs and bacon with—oh my ears and whiskers!—muffins. Than which nothing ought to be more Brit, but where do you find muffins in Britain? Not anyway in old Islington.

Eggs over once lightly, sunny side up, half an eye open.

"Be it ever so redolent, there's no place like . . ."

Li'l ol' Rock. I stepped out past emporia, airways offices, banks. All shut. Cars like ocean liners, desultory passers-by hefting the tonnage of Sunday newspapers, dogs on the leash, all these I refrained from greeting, though tempted. The sparse pedestrians were sober citizens of our epoch, ready for church. The exception was the ol'-timer I was about to pass on the next street corner. Black hat, corn cob, station there by the tourist office, he was straight from the pages of *National Geographic*, an off-duty Santa doubling as Walt Whitman. He ought to have been whittling.

"Morning, squire," I greeted him, hurrying on before he drew his bowie knife.

A touch of the manics never hurt anyone. Sunshine was going to fight its way through or I was no prognosticator.

Nonetheless I kept an eye out for muggers and bowie knives. This wasn't London, where, to be coshed, you had to be in uniform in Brixton, or an Asian on the tube, or a pensioner. Four hundred anonymous murders a week here in the States, last figure I saw. If you missed those, seventy screen murders on the box any day of the week, not counting cowboys and Indians.

Lawdy, those muffins! I'd take a crateful back. Miriam would mutter about calories, but finally she'd drool. Sam would roll in them. O butter-clogged muffins!

I stepped through the glass doors of my hotel and into the hall porter, who said, "Hi, good breakfast?"

"A humdinger," I said.

"Yeah?" He nodded in the direction of a black man lounging on a settee. "Police to see you."

Bobby Foster, natch.

"Identification's not the problem anymore. We've got prints from ten years back. But the Reverend's got money. With the lawyers he'd hire we need more than prints. Can you imagine it, Henry, the faithful in their thousands on their knees outside the courthouse, singing his praises?"

Henry. In Hyde Park, wearing his BAGS hat, he'd come on strong with "sir." Now we were buddied. Colleagues anyway.

"Pinkerton's?" I'd hazarded.

"Who?" he'd said, baffled.

We sat in the back of a yellow taxi which bore us past the banks and stores I'd just walked by. In spite of Agent Foster's urgings, next the flashing of his shield, the driver declined to progress so much as a hair above the fifteen-mile-an-hour limit.

"Officer, I gotta wife, four kids, and this cab," the driver said. "You want to speed, you take your squad car."

I'd a feeling Foster's impatience might've been due to my leisurely breakfast, and he was letting me know it without actually coming out and saying so. Evidently the gospel singers were required to assemble one hour before the service, and he was going to be late. I was inclined to point out that if I'd known he'd be turning up for me, I'd have been waiting.

"You haven't talked to him yet?" he inquired in his gravy-brown voice.

"The Reverend?"

"The reporter."

Keeping Ramsden in one piece had been the burden of this bloke's song in Hyde Park. Was he still on with the same song?

"Only just arrived," I told him. "Don't even know where he's staying."

"The Arkansas Traveller. Except he's gone, he didn't sleep there, and his room's wrecked. Driver?" Foster leaned forward. "Thought I'd mention it. We're in a thirty-mile-an-hour zone."

"Starts at the next stoplight," the driver said. "See the sign? I'll pull over, you can take a picture."

Foster leaned back. He had on his lap a zip-up grip which I supposed held his singer's robe. All I'd gleaned so far was that he was with the Little Rock field division of the FBI, he'd been investigating Jody James for five months, and those cognizant were the FBI and my AC at the Yard. A question of courtesy, and the green light, my assistant commissioner, Foster said.

And now me. Since July, he said, he'd been a BAGS singer. Five months.

"Too damn late," he muttered.

Even muttering, the voice throbbed, threatening to steam up the windows. Whether too late to see Ramsden alive again, or too late to file onstage for this next, imminent, born-again shindig, I wasn't clear.

I said, "Mind giving me a hint?" If this were the FBI investigating, the Reverend's villainy had to be a violation of federal law. Whatever federal laws were, I'd never had cause to study them. Sabotage, I guessed. Espionage. Kidnapping. Sending disagreeable material and matériel through the post, whether bombs or filthy pictures. "Tax?"

"He can't be nailed on tax, Henry." I'd not yet decided whether to call him Bobby at the first opportunity, or never in my life. "Churches," he said, "don't show their books. We've a constitutional guarantee exempting them. Ask what the champagne cost, they'll play their religious freedom card, and ask you right back, 'Who questions the Pope's expense account?' ''

That out of the way, he proceeded with more than a hint of the Reverend's villainy. I wondered if the cab's hurtling at very nearly thirty miles an hour hadn't encouraged him. With one eye on the cabby he lowered his voice, but its reverberations were still around force ten, rattling the windows.

Jody C. James had been born John Frederick Kolb in Kansas City. Mother a dancer, father unknown. Umpteen aliases between John Frederick Kolb and Jody C. James, and through half a dozen southern states every kind of trouble from vagrancy to embezzlement, assault, and stolen property offences. He'd escaped spells in the slammer—Mr. Foster's word—by what appeared to have been the purest luck of coming up before religious-minded judges who'd been impressed by his gift for biblical quotation, respectful manner, and holy expression. He'd dropped out of sight, then surfaced seven years ago, shortly after four Arabs had lost their lives at Pithley, as a preacher, with a flair for publicity and enough cash to buy staff and air time. The connections between this rising star of the electric church and dead Arabs far away, if there were a connection, had been made one year earlier by a semiretired clerk in FBI records, a born-again zealot who watched Sunday morning television. He'd been going through mouldering files prior to shovelling them into the cellar when he'd seen in the Pithley file the description of the chauffeur-courier with an American accent.

I nodded sagely. I wondered if there mightn't have been another element in the phenomenon of Our 'Enry as temporary God Squad, apart from Miriam. Such as the Factory's brass grubbing in our own files and finding that the geezers who'd liaised with Somerset had been Terry Sutton and me.

I'd not have said no to Terry's company now. The cheerfulness of half an hour ago had evaporated. Ramsden not having slept at his hotel was discouraging.

"The carpenter's shop isn't total make-believe," Foster was saying. "He worked as a carpenter here in '74. He used to go round with a Bible telling people it was the whole truth and nothing but the truth. The religious dimension checks out right down the line. Before he tried making it as a carpenter he was hustling tourists in Richmond and Atlanta, showing them the churches. What do you do with a guy who'll kill if that's what it takes to spread the gospel?" He looked moodily through the window at fleeing blocks of flats, and now a park. The road was tree-lined, the speed limit up to forty. "Ramsden's the reporter who had the squabble with the chauffeur ferrying the Arabs, right? Now he's deep into the First Born-Again Church of God. Is it too much to hope he's got proof the chauffeur's the Reverend?"

"If he had we'd have read it in the *Post*."

"After the Homecoming Awakening, we find him, Henry. Talk to him. If he can talk. Then you take him back home. Out of it."

"He's not going home without a story. I can't force him. He came for a story."

"You believe that?"

"No."

"Damned right." He was looking at his watch. "If all he ever wanted was a story he'd have been given one— God bless you, son, come back and see us. If he wanted a story about the Reverend wasting four Arabs, my guess is we'd never have seen him again. But if he already has the story, something that stands up, all the evidence, and he isn't writing it, that makes sense of our Reverend's crapping about with a bruising here, a mauling there, threats, indecision." Now he was winding the watch, which wasn't the variety that keeps going untouched through all eternity. There was even a face with hands, and numbers from one to twelve. "How much would you guess Ramsden's asking?"

I shrugged. I'd no idea, not then, any more than I'd have guessed that the chauffeur who'd disposed of the sheiks might be Jody. Jody as a target for blackmail, on the other hand, and Ramsden as blackmailer, that hadn't

been difficult. Whether booze, bums, bookies, or stashing
BAGS funds under his mattress—murder, I admit it, I'd
not considered—the Reverend had everything to lose and
the money to pay. Ramsden's tracking after him had pro-
duced nothing sensational for the *Post*, only pain for
Ramsden, who'd kept on tracking anyway, and writing
nothing. More as if he were trying to get through to the
Reverend, trying to tell him something, rather than digging
up the dirt.

How much money was he demanding, that was mildly
intriguing. How did an amateur blackmailer arrive at a
figure? Come to that, how did a professional?

You could hardly leave it up to the victim. There'd been
guesses in the press at the income of Jody's born-again
church, but they were guesses. Even if you knew what the
Reverend was personally worth, did you charge what the
market would bear, or tread more gently? A modest sum
might be paid over immediately, gratefully even. Further
installments to be arranged.

I couldn't even decide whether, as worries went, this
wouldn't be a blackmailer's blackest, fixing the price—
keeping him awake at night, driving him to the bottle, or
his sweetest.

"Stop just up ahead there, my friend's getting out,"
Foster told the driver.

Was it something I'd said?

"Sorry, Henry, I can't be seen showing up with you.
It's only half a mile. Try thumbing a ride. One o'clock,
your hotel, okay?"

"Okay, Bobby."

The taxi drew up at the side of a broad avenue flanked
by woods. A sign proclaimed, "The First Born-Again
Church of God Welcomes Godly Drivers." Distantly ahead
awaited silvery buildings in green spaces. Traffic streamed
past.

"If anyone asked me," I said, hand on the door handle,
"I'd say the FBI were bloody lucky to infiltrate that
choir."

"Don't believe it. Took eight months. I was the twelfth
to audition."

"First black?"

"Right. Right time, right place, right colour. The Reverend was expanding his ethnic image."

I didn't try hitchhiking. Still half an hour before curtain-up. Not that not hitchhiking was easy. Cars slowed, offering me a ride, one driver called to me, "Hey there, brother in Jesus!" Receding bumper stickers beseeched me to be born again. I concentrated on Miriam and Sam. The sun was a poorly focussed, lemonade-coloured splash in the sky.

The road passed through a surrealist frame which framed nothing and reminded me of my notion of the entrance to a Texas ranch, though this frame wasn't timber but steel, or aluminium, something metallic, and the gargantuan neon sign above, instead of revealing that here was the Lazy Y, announced, "Creation World." Flat, grubby land reached away on all sides, crisscrossed by tracks and gravel roads, fringed by horizons of woods. Where the ground had not yet been churned brown by bulldozers, occasional green scrub sprouted. Cranes and cement mixers, guarded by pyramids of sand, awaited Monday morning. Beyond a concrete wilderness packed with cars gleamed the silver domes, turrets, honeycombed arches, and precipitously angled roofs of Creation World, as much of it as had been built, which looked a fair amount.

Without in the least wanting to feel crabby before I'd even got there, I had a dispiriting impression of avantgarde design cribbed from the last space film but one, and already stale as a bun. The crowds beyond the parking were getting on for Epsom Derby dimensions. The closer I approached, the more the scene took on a bank holiday air, though the people were sombrely dressed, with some families just standing, some buying doughnuts, others pursuing signs pointing them to the Hall of Creation, Souvenir Citadel, Genesis City, and the church itself, presumably the domed building lapped by green lawns.

Aiming for the church, murmuring, "Excuse me . . . sorry," I edged between families. From loudspeakers floated a gospel song:

"Like the pilot of a plane
The fireman of a train . . ."

Along a thronged path between lawns. Up stone slabs of
steps, more slowly, wedged in a press of mufflered Christians. Then carpeted steps where the churchgoers were so
numerous that progress came virtually to a stop. At the
head of the steps redcoats examined tickets.

In the lobby beyond the redcoats I glimpsed the paraphernalia of stands selling records and born-again wam-
pum. We inched forward towards wafts of central heating.
The smell was overcoats, after shave, and vanilla, though
heaven knows where the vanilla came from, unless the
doughnuts. Here on the brink of the First Born-Again
Church of God, the Reverend James's sanctum, his hymn
to God, sobriety had possessed the faithful. They spoke in
whispers and answered one another with awed nods.

"We're on our way—
Born again!"

"Ticket, sir?"

"Press, I said, smiling back.

"Not," said into my ear another voice, "the police?"

Breathing into this other ear was the gent with the
missing chin I'd had the contretemps with in Manchester,
the girl-slapper, smiling now of course, but breathless,
probably from having sprinted, and indisputably inquiring
whether I wasn't police rather than press.

"Right," I said. "*Police Gazette*. Features, foreign
news—"

"Ticket holders only, sir. Every seat's taken. We can
offer closed-circuit television in the Calvary Lounge, or
network in the Noah Room. Down the steps, to your left,
past the restaurant."

I thought it a good idea not to argue. Apart from there
being too many red jackets, I wasn't at all sure I wanted to
attend another of the Reverend's services. Ramsden was
hardly going to be there, taking notes. The only reason for
him being at Creation World at all, far as I could see,

would be by appointment to collect, which might be before or after the service, but hardly during. I wasn't certain I wanted to watch the service on telly, except to say wotcher to Bobby Foster, see whether he'd made it in time. I trod back down the steps.

Past the restaurant. Mess of pottage, eight dollars? I'd mention pottage to Miriam. Might go down a treat with her archæologists.

I didn't choose the Calvary Lounge, which sounded depressing by comparison with the possibly *gemütlich* Noah Room. Being close and impeccably signposted, the Calvary Lounge chose me. Rows of chairs, every one occupied, had been drawn up in front of a screen which filled most of one wall. Filling an adjacent wall was a multicoloured painting of Christ crucified, staggeringly impressive in its vulgarity, at least to my eyes. Somewhere between a poster commissioned from an art student high on Dali and a blown-up print from Boots.

I took up a position among other latecomers against a third wall, whereupon a teen-age siren in a red jacket appeared offering me booklets. I shook my head. The amplified sound, jet-plane level, was the organ relayed from the church. On the screen the gospel singers were filing redly onto a stage loud with flags, gold and silver drapes, a banner blazoning "Homecoming Awakening," and a photo of the Reverend James of the brazen dimensions people use when they want your vote.

Hi there, Bobby!

> "Born again for Jesus!
> Born again for God!"

Even here, in front of a screen, the viewers were on their feet, singing, whooping, and hand-clapping with a verve which left the born-again British congregations about as effusive as a Quaker meeting. Jody was home. The cameras interspersed shots of the campaign stage and its chorus line, singing out, with the whooping congregation. This being closed circuit, at least we'd be spared the commercials.

Spared? Much more of this and I'd be pleading for commercials. In the congregation streamers unfurled and balloons floated, carnival jollity contrasting with Sunday suits and dresses. Was the razzmatazz for Jesus, Jody, or for its own sake? Watching the singers, I was a fair time deciding what was different about them.

The bony, shock-headed girl wasn't there was what. Petal Merchant. At that time I'd never heard her name, merely noticed her, in Manchester and at the Albert Hall.

More trying than even the stereophonic sound was the suffocating heat. I fanned myself with my hat. Though I looked round for a bar, pretty clearly there wasn't going to be one.

> "Count, count, count,
> On the Man at the Wheel . . ."

Everyone knew it, everyone sang.

When the cameras wandered over the congregation I kept an eye out for Ramsden. I didn't see him.

When the Reverend strode spotlit onstage you'd have supposed he'd been voted President, such stamping and hollering, like film clips you see of rodeos.

When he lifted his arms high, one hand holding the Bible, and opened his mouth to speak, the tumult increased.

"Friends, dear friends . . ." Whooping, caterwauling. "Good, born-again friends of Arkansas . . ."

Clamorous applause rendered null any progress he might've been making in subduing the racket.

"Jesus told Nicodemus"—the name Jesus acted like a code word for quiet—" 'Except a man be born again, he cannot see the kingdom of God.' "

He had silence. His eyes were closed. "And the Lord said, 'How long halt ye between two—' "

Opinions, he was presumably going to say, but the end of the sentence was lost because someone else had started talking. Shouting, I should say, and none too clearly. Poor Reverend James, who'd had silence for all of five seconds.

He looked startled, as well he might. Everyone was startled. A demonstration here in the very cradle, one of them anyway, of born-again Christendom, where every ticket holder probably had to be a screened, registered, born-again Christian? Unthinkable. Certainly, I'd have thought, unprecedented.

'' . . . killer, murderer! Jody James, murderer! Tell us about it, Jody! Tell us about the murders, Jody! Tell us—''

The camera had picked up Ramsden standing on a chair in the congregation, mouthing hysterically. Recognising him as Ramsden wasn't easy because his face was a pumpkin which had been dropped from a height. But the accent shouted from the dough mouth was English, not American.

Anyway, couldn't have been anyone else, could it?

Like the Reverend, Ramsden wasn't allowed to finish what he'd been saying either. Redcoats clawed him down. I stuck my hat on my head and barged from the Calvary Room.

THIRTEEN

What you do is go limp. I know a fair amount about these matters. Anyone whose student days included the odd sit-in, anyone in the least politically oriented, that's to say, knows that coppers aren't going to rough you up unless you struggle, which some of them prefer you to do because that gives them an excuse. What they do when they get you out of the public gaze and into the wagon might well be something else. But on site, so to speak, if you simply flop there's not much they can do except pick you up and carry you off.

Same with this lot. The cameras were on them. So that's what I did, and that's what they did, smilingly picking up the rubbish and hefting it out, four of them, one to each limb.

". . . who the devil has deranged may still be worthy of the love that Jesus . . . " Jody was announcing into his mike, cashing in, exploiting to the hilt the little local disturbance. Phoney, hypocritical, evil bastard.

Not that he mightn't have been sincere in guessing I was deranged. Anyone standing up in that congregation and spouting about the Reverend as a killer must've been whacko. Presumably it's medically possible for a clobbering such as I'd had in my hotel room, the night before, to loosen whatever bits of the brain look after judgement?

Derangement didn't come into it though. Despair perhaps, but I knew what I was doing. For me this was the end so far as the Reverend and his mobsters were concerned. I'd had them, up to here, the whole shebang. The cameras were on me, primed and humming, or they would be, awaiting the exposure of Jody at last, chapter and verse.

The pity was that I hadn't been more coherent. There hadn't been time. They never gave me a chance. The redcoat who had my left leg was Chunky, and if I'd spat when he turned his head to look at me, as he kept doing, I might've got him in the eye.

But I didn't spit, because now was pacifism time. The Gandhi tactic.

As I plainly hadn't the least intention of fighting back, as no one possibly could've been limper, in the lobby they set me on my feet. They encouraged me to walk, steering me towards the door into the vestry, or torture chamber, or whatever it was going to be. Other reasons for putting me down may have been, first, the expulsion of a bashed-up head case as if he were a sack of trash being bad public relations, and second, they were tired.

I was tired too. Everyone was tired. But they shouldn't have put me down. Coppers don't put you down until they've got you in the wagon. I sidestepped behind Chunky, jinked in front of the redcoat to my right, and ran.

I honestly don't think I expected to get halfway across the lobby, let alone as far as the steps down to the outside. The best I hoped for was that the cameras had followed me, and were getting it all down for the next television news, and Jody's trial. I hadn't even had time to reflect that under pressure what I did have was, if not grace, two still unbroken legs which not so long ago, in Hyde Park, had sped me off like a rabbit.

The first obstacle was either a matron in furs or a polar bear, one of the polar bears down for the day from the Ozarks. I'd achieved all of four strides and was gathering speed. I didn't get much of a look. She went down with a shriek.

The second obstacle was a table piled with records. This I had to skirt, not being a hurdler. Giving the tower of records a tap as I fled by didn't delay me for an instant and may have caused the redcoats to watch where they were stepping. Beatified records at twelve dollars apiece, after all. Though I doubt they went so far as to help pick them up.

I didn't look back. Down the steps, five, six at a time. Along the side of the church, dodging startled mums, dads, and bantlings, and round the corner for the car park ahead and my rented car. With luck. If strewn records impeded them, or they were natural slow coaches. This time I had my clothes plus car keys.

Someone had removed the car park. In front was grass, glassy buildings, and people meandering, or standing listening to the Reverend's praying, relayed through *al fresco* loudspeakers. Not a car to be seen. As well as the brain cells which govern judgement, the beating had flattened my bump of direction.

I dashed for the nearest refuge. Open doors into what resembled an outsize igloo. "Hall of Evolution," proclaimed winking fairground lights.

"Ramsden!" somewhere a voice shouted.

Not my father, or any friend of my childhood, come to lift me away. I charged through the doors, past gawpers, a uniform, a cash desk, onward round and through mobs of visitors, optimistic there would be exits at the igloo's end.

Where redcoats could be waiting.

Not yet though, possibly. Though if I hung about, the place would be crawling with them, inside and out.

I accelerated, swerving, dodging. At the end of the hall, beyond the assembled heads, I'd already seen a sign— "Way Out."

"Sorry . . . excuse me . . ."

While not pausing to take notes, I had the impression that the sole exhibit in the Hall of Evolution was the cage in the centre of the hall, and above it, writ large, the inquiry "Are These Your Ancestors?" I glimpsed a furry something in the cage. Chimp, gibbon, blue-bottomed mandrill, one of those. There may have been a family of them. The squash of visitors blocked my view.

Anyway, a good joke, very risible, Your Pastorship.

Through the exit, into watery sunlight, and no redcoats. The car park would now be to the right—would it? Too far

in front for me to read stood a signpost with a dozen arms.
I ran towards it.

". . . in England where I found true faith and, also, I
grieve to say, troubled souls, side by side, dear friends
. . ." the Reverend was booming in his chattier style.

The Homecoming Awakening service was flogging on.
Was deranged Ramsden forgotten then? Had the word
gone out to ignore him?

"Ramsden!"

In the opposite direction from where the Ramsden shouter
was shouting, I spied red. I raced past the signpost, past
commissionaires outside Genesis City, and queues and
uniforms inside, ignoring complainings, slapping away a
vexed hand, and stumbling into blackness where vibrated a
voice which was not, I thought, the Reverend's. I cracked
my shin against something and swore.

"Ssssh!" hissed the public.

". . . he made the stars also . . ." intoned a voice.

Genesis City was black only here at ground level. Even
here, groping with outstretched arms, I dimly made out an
arena of seated spectators, as in a planetarium. Above, in
the dome, lights twinkled.

". . . God set them in the firmament of the heaven
. . ." droned the disembodied voice, very sonorously.

I tried to hurry, groping round this rear, circling row of
seats, hunting a way out.

Short of reaching my car, I saw no solution. Outside in
the open, aimlessly running, couldn't help but close in
disaster. In the church, the show went on but I was unable
to believe I was being ignored. By now every steward in
Creation World would be searching. They'd be posted at
fifty compass points.

Inside, in exhibition halls and hot-dog parlours, the
respite might be worth five minutes. They could turn up
the lights and come for me. They could simply wait outside. I've have to leave sometime.

Give up then? Lie down with folded arms? I'd done
virtually that already, in the church. So what had I gained
by running? What was changed?

I was free was what. Sod all of them.

Standing up there in the church, trying to tell it as it was, I'd been unhinged. If they wrapped their hands round me once more, it'd be the last time. For ever. Jody would make sure of that. He'd got no choice.

Me or him.

A dozen paces ahead, an exit. Now the domed roof was awash with heaving blue sea and thrashing fish. Though we didn't need it explained, the sonorous voice was explaining it anyway.

". . . God created great whales, and every living creature that moveth . . ."

"Ramsden, for God's sake!" whispered a voice from an inch away.

Apart from him being barely visible in the gloom, even at this kissing distance, I'm not positive I'd have recognised him. Possibly the hat was the giveaway. Our previous meetings had been, to put it mildly, casual. We'd never been introduced. At that time I didn't even know his name, though I'd guessed he was a policeman.

". . . evening and morning were the fifth day . . ."

"They've got bloody guns," whispered the policeman. One of his hands was bunching the lapels of my coat. "Chrissake, stop buggering about, you're coming with me—"

"Ssssh!" hissed the great unwashed in the nearer seats.

"—you poxy, horrible hack—"

His gasp when I punched his face elicited an encore of sibilants from the audience. But he let go of my coat, so I ran for the exit, and through it into a lighted foyer bristling with exits, entrances, arrows, and directions I didn't stop to study. None was likely to point me to the car park. I ran along a glass corridor which at its end, I fancifully imagined, ought to have sported passports, baggage, and customs signs. There should've been girls with bright airways eyes and forage caps directing me to my plane, and home. Instead, I was decanted into another foyer with, so far as I could see, no door to the outside.

I saw commissionaires, disorganised queues, slow-motion milling. Always and still I was in Creation World, the real world, hunted by redcoats. I looked back. Along the glass corridor the copper galloped.

Queue-pusher Ramsden queue-pushed. He was the expert, sick as a cat, by now sobbing aloud, I think, though hereabouts memory grows fuzzy. I thumped a uniform holding out a hand for my ticket and stumbled into Madame Tussaud's, scattering customers. I recall my irrelevant sense of surprise that none of the scattered should have retaliated with more than cries of indignation. Maybe it's the influence of old Hollywood movies on the box, but I'd always supposed Americans took unkindly to being jostled, the ethos being all men are born equal so don't jostle me, buster. I couldn't imagine Spencer Tracy being jostled with impunity. This crowd was weakly human, doing nothing, though that may've been because I was gone before they had the chance.

Madame Tussaud's it wasn't. If only. Dear God, being home I'd not have said no to! But everywhere were wax figures. At Creation World there'd had to be a waxworks. Here it was.

The Hall of Fame? Unless I shifted, another few seconds and for me it was going to be the pluperfect Hall of Fame. Wax, flesh, and blood, everything, all in the past tense.

A hoyden in a bikini holding aloft a blood-smeared, bearded head blurred past. A more trimly bearded face with starched, white-robed body attached stood with a loaf of bread in one palm, a fish in the other.

Hall of Fame, New Testament. O attentive swat Ramsden, scholar, top of your scripture classes! A mighty centrepiece of four rearing, snorting horses slowed me practically to a stop.

I didn't have much choice. They reared and snorted almost from wall to wall.

Riders rode the horses. Either I could go round, which was the long way, or through, risking cracking my skull on a fetlock.

I went through. On the way I reached up and helped myself to the sword brandished by the rider on the red horse. The other horses were white, black, and I suppose pale. A kind of beige anyway, though I wasn't looking too closely. In any event, indisputably I was traversing the

New Testament waxworks. Apocalypse now, then, and for always.

When I say I helped myself, that's misleading, because it wasn't exactly as easy as pie. It was quick, if it hadn't been I'd have given up, dashed on, because I wasn't going to hang about. But the sword didn't just slide out of the horseman's hand. It didn't slide at all. At the second tug the whole thing rocked, horse and rider, while through prancing legs, beyond flanks and shanks, paying customers began boringly to squeal. If I hadn't left off tugging, eventually it would've all come down, the whole monstrous red sculpture, probably bringing with it the black, the white, and the pale. I was beyond caring, and assisted by a thump from my fist, at the third tug the sword was mine, and with it the horseman's red hand, wrist, half a forearm, and a cloud of plaster.

One of the trivial questions likely to be put to me when I give evidence, as I assume I'll have to, will be, why the vandalism? Why borrow the sword? I'd only be able to answer, because it was there. Possibly that I might defend myself with it, slashing it this way and that. A weighty, two-edged, yard and a half of sword it was, steel I'd have thought, sooner than painted plaster or wax. Without testing it on a steward, I couldn't have said. My impression was that it was blunt as a banana. The blunter the better because any moment, running again, jinking, lugging the sword, I was likely to trip and go down in a nasty, bloodletting tangle with it.

Out into sunlight. I stared about me in an effort to find my bearings. I was on a strip of patio between flashy buildings, the calm little disturbed by the handful of wanderers, or the gospel singing which carried through the Arkansas morning. Then, from heaven knows where, a brace of redcoats were heading towards me.

No guns. At least that. Unless they had them up their jumpers.

When I began to run, they ran. I aimed across the patio to the nearest doors opposite, lugging the imbecile sword. One of the redcoats slowed, stopped, and blew a whistle. The one who'd kept running reached the doors before I did

and turned towards me in a crouch, arms spread out,
filling the entrance. He didn't have to open his mouth for
me to recognise him, but he did open it, or started to, and
there was a glint of gold molar. Whether he was going to
say, "Your ticket please, sir," or was drawing breath
before charging, I never found out. There are moments,
experience has taught me, when one must act at once if
one is to act at all. I swung the sword two-handed.

It wasn't easy to swing, and almost impossible to aim
with any accuracy, there being no proper grip. You had to
hold the horseman's hand and broken forearm. I aimed for
the redcoat's shoulder with the flat of the blade. But he
was coming towards me in his crouch, bobbing, and I may
have hit him higher up. I didn't see. What with the sweat,
tears perhaps, and in my head pandemonium, I wasn't
seeing anything clearly. One moment he was there, blocking the doorway, and the next moment the doorway was
clear. Through the door were stairs which I climbed, not
nimbly, dragging the sword.

Then a corridor. I think what I was looking for was a
window through which I'd see the car park. So far as I was
thinking at all by this stage, I believe I continued to think
of my car as the only haven. I opened a door which let me
into an empty, brightly lit room smelling of socks and
showers after a football game.

I bolted the door behind me. In place of windows the
room had benches and rows of lockers. Through the din of
gospel singing I could hear the choking, whimpering noises
I was making, which probably was as well for my morale,
what remained of it, for they were evidence that at least I
was still alive. There sounded hammering on the door I'd
locked, and shouts from the corridor.

I took down one of the red angel robes which hung on
the wall and dragged it on. True, my memory of much of
this remains hazy. I know I wasn't exactly lucid about
what I was up to. And yet, looking back, the robe was not
so fatuous as all that. Wouldn't any camouflage be better
than none if I were to make it to my car? Conceivably, if
only for moments, I might be taken for a BAGS singer on
an urgent mission, one who'd received a telegram, or was

off to collect music sheets. Moments might make all the difference.

Ideally the robe would've had a Ku Klux Klan hood, or at least a cowl, but it didn't, and too bad. I hesitated before picking up the sword. The corniness of the spectacle I must've presented, red-robed, holding the sword, was so extreme I wanted to laugh. I believe I may have done so, though if I did, I've no wish to remember the sound of that laugh.

God's avenging angel. Symbolic Ramsden. I opened the door at the far end of the BAGS green room. Whether this artistes' room had been for men or women I'd not observed, and it scarcely mattered, the robes being presumably unisex. I stepped into a dazzle of gold and silver curtains.

I could still have turned back. But to what? From the other side of the gold and silver sang, *fortissimo*, the choir. The congregation sang. They clapped and whooped, undismayed by the disagreeable little scene when the nice stewards had carried out the nut. Unless he'd joined the hunt, and he hadn't because he'd been preaching through the loudspeakers, Jody too stood somewhere on the other side of the curtains.

> "He'll cure your hang-ups
> He'll calm your fears . . ."

I trod behind the curtains, plucking at them, looking for a way through, trailing Excalibur.

Why I hadn't realised it before was because I was in a state. Anyone would've been. I've explained all that. But anyway I realised it now. One refuge more secure than the car, probably the only secure refuge in all Creation World, was out there onstage. Particularly if stewards were carrying guns.

Guns, for pity's sake! All right, this was gun-happy America. But I don't think I ever believed the policeman's mention of guns. I never took it in. I was more ready to believe that the London bobby was under strain, as I was, and hallucinating. From what you hear, they reckon themselves overworked.

The gap I found in the curtains brought me onstage behind the seventh or eighth singer from the right. That's stage right, about where Petal would've been if she'd been there.

I could've squeezed into the line-up. Joined the choir. It occurred to me. But I didn't know the words.

"Excuse me," I said, stepping between singers, onto and over the platform. I advanced towards the footlights.

I should've left the sword behind, of course, but that didn't occur to me. You don't think of everything. I don't know whether they reasoned at the time, the stewards, that the sword would give them an excuse. Perhaps not. But their lawyers aren't likely to forget it.

The congregation, front rows illumined by the lights onstage, reached away into gloom, then into darkness at the back of the auditorium. They were singing well. Heaven knows what they made of this apparition with the sword. There was scattered applause, not so thunderous as to bring down the roof, but whoops and cheers from those, I suppose, who imagined I was part of the performance, some novelty imported perhaps from the Great Awakening in Britain, the point of which shortly would be revealed to them. Jody I noticed stage left in his Bible-clasped-to-the-bosom stance. His eyes were closed.

Well, no great hurry. He'd be aware of me in a moment.

I raised an arm for quiet. I might've raised both arms, presidential-style, but one was anchored by a half hundred-weight of sword. The weird truth is, I think, that in those seconds I was enjoying myself, or almost.

Because I wasn't myself. Unless you're a hopeless, shy introvert with stage fright, the stage has this heady, dreamy, transforming effect. It does for me. You have to be a show-off. If you are, then when you're up there onstage, hamming your role, you're not yourself, and that was why I was close to elation, because considering the circumstances—the place, time, and somewhere the redcoats—the last person I wanted to be was Peter Ramsden.

I expect I was going to try to tell them once more about the real Jody. Jody, the Man and the Myth. I don't know, I had nothing rehearsed. It would've made no difference if

I had because for the second time I was given no time. A redcoat carrying a shotgun was running down the aisle.

He'd come out of the far dark, into the gloom, and was running over bright carpet towards the stage, and the idiot with the sword stage-centre.

"Count, count, count . . ."

One certainty was that the gospel singers hadn't been programmed for this. They sang on, but raggedly, as if undecided whether to keep going or stop and await fresh instructions.

"Ramsden!" cried somewhere a familiar Cockney cry.

Jody dropped to his knees. To pray, I assumed at the time, though now, looking back, I suspect he was ducking. He probably finished flat on his face with his hands over his head. I didn't notice because my attention was on the redcoat, Chinless, who'd halted in the aisle a few rows short of the front row. He was very well illumined. He lifted his gun to his shoulder and pointed it—unbelievably—at me.

Quite possibly he never intended to fire. No one will ever know. I'd have thought his purpose would've been to scare me into shutting up, and coming along quietly, and what I do know is he'd have succeeded, but he wasn't given the chance. A robed singer who'd left the line-up was advancing fast downstage, raising in his black hand a rival gun, a pistol.

Simultaneously, the copper in the hat who'd been for ever yelling my name crashed into me with the sort of body tackle which elicits delirium at Cardiff Arms Park.

Too late. In the same instant, Chinless fired, and Babby Faster, my acquaintance from the restaurant at the Tudor Inn, he of the ripe bass, fired too, his bullet removing the top of the redcoat's head.

So I'm told. I didn't see it, I'm happy to say. I doubt my Cockney copper did either, both of us being enmeshed in each other, and Excalibur, and shot, heaped beside the footlights.

FOURTEEN

Pamela, jewel, got your bag packed? Where's it to be? The two of us. Rio, Acapulco, you choose. Girl of my dreams.

First, I've listened to Peter Ramsden's tapes. Here are my first unconsidered comments.

Whether they'll be much different when I've considered, I don't know. I doubt it.

Everything he said stands up, close enough to make no difference, up to his account of the meeting in St. Paul's with the Reverend James.

The dental plate and tooth which he left at the back of Dr. Johnson's statue, that was true. The tooth's gone to the Yard, according to Mister Agent Foster. Forensics should know shortly if it's the Reverend's, if they don't already. Tracing the dentist's going to take longer. My guess is the Reverend will be sent down for life, unless he gets a born-again judge.

If this false tooth doesn't match up with the one Ramsden picked out of his knuckle, nothing matches up, and I give up. But why, if it doesn't match up, would Jody be so fussed about the squeeze from a wretched, yellow press reporter? Why not ignore him, or tell the police? He'll have to be more convincing in court than he is onstage to talk his way out of this. He'll not be preaching to the converted in court.

Foster was first to hear Ramsden's tapes. He got onto the Yard about the tooth. He's several jumps ahead of me.

He's not jumping though. He's limping. He was hit in the left leg and he's got a crutch. I'm not laughing, mean to say, it's not amusing, it must be very painful, a limping situation like that. But at least he's up and about, which is more than some of us.

Right, Ramsden's account of the St. Paul's rendezvous. Fine as far as it went. What he omitted to mention was that it was then he put the squeeze on the Reverend. Must've been. They didn't meet again, not eyeball to eyeball.

Foster was in St. Paul's. He watched the Reverend and Ramsden sitting, talking. What I'm wondering is if the Reverend didn't agree to pay up, but couldn't manage it in London, and told Ramsden he'd have to come to Little Rock. The loot was in the First National City, or First City National, and there was no way of transferring it to London. What's called playing for time.

In his Hampstead flat, with Petal, Ramsden lied by omission there too. Something was agreed. Did he enlist Petal as go-between between himself and the Reverend? Did he tell her the Reverend was worth money to him, to them both, and chew over with her how much he should ask, what she'd accept as her cut?

Lies, too, in his account of his session with Petal in his Arkansas Traveller room. All along, what Ramsden was after wasn't a story for the *Post*, or his first book. Not primarily. It was blackmailing Jody James.

When I say all along, that's to say from when he first thought of it. That'd be after he filched the Reverend's case and found the tooth. That was evidence. He thought he was home and dry. Pay off his debts, money for life, and bugger the posh newspapers that hadn't wanted him.

Unimportant, but I'm not sure I believe he bedded Petal Merchant either. I'm not saying he wouldn't have tried, or she was lily-white impregnable. Anything but. But judging from the tapes, and the opinion of Madam Goodenough, his news editor, she of the double gins, he liked seeing himself as the big macho lover, and he'd have had no objection to others sharing that assessment.

The steward he hit with the sword, the one who tried to stop him getting into the church through the back, he was decapitated, as good as. I'm not positive Ramsden wasn't fibbing there too. I can believe he may not have been aware of what he'd done, but only if I try very hard.

Ramsden died just after four o'clock this morning. Foster's getting the details. Whether it was expected or a surprise I've not managed to make out. I gather the sword did more damage than the shotgun, but I'd thought he was recovering. Pulmonary embolism is all I've heard, whatever that is.

Apparently it wasn't just his stomach. Most of his legs were gone, blown away—not just broken. And his manhood. Perhaps he's better off now.

The girl's vanished and with her a quarter of a million dollars. None of my affair. Reading between Foster's resonant vowels, I'd hazard not too much police time's going to be spent looking for her.

Why would it? Stop Press—"BAGS Singer Nicks BAGS Funds." An internal matter, as we say. Unless a church member lays a complaint. I'd have thought the First Born-Again Church of God would be suffering enough disarray without trying to cope with complaints.

Wouldn't surprise me if some of the stewards started looking for her though. Wherever she is, she'd probably do well to invest some of her booty in a heavy lock and several Doberman pinschers.

Pamela, light of my life, that's it. Got it all? Commas and colons in place? You could react now, lay your hand on my fevered brow, but only if you really want to.

Actually, old girl, I think its not all that fevered. Know what the doctor said this morning, the one with the frozen fingers? I said, "Doctor, am I out of danger yet?" He said, "What danger?"

So I said, "You mean no more daily bulletins?" And he said, "What daily bulletins? What in hell are you talking about?"

Cheeky bugger.

Pamela, mavourneen, fix me another call to London, would you, the Islington number? Just to say hello.

If the hospital management's getting stroppy, reverse the charges. Collect, that what you say? It'll be all right. Sam'll pay.